Hello Golden Gate

Goodbye Russia

A Young Girl's Odyssey From the Far East to the New World

A Memoir by Olga Valcoff

Bloomington, IN   Milton Keynes, UK

AuthorHouse™
1663 Liberty Drive, Suite 200
Bloomington, IN 47403
www.authorhouse.com
Phone: 1-800-839-8640

AuthorHouse™ UK Ltd.
500 Avebury Boulevard
Central Milton Keynes, MK9 2BE
www.authorhouse.co.uk
Phone: 08001974150

© 2007 Olga Valcoff. All rights reserved.

No part of this book may be reproduced, stored in a retrieval system, or transmitted by any means without the written permission of the author.

First published by AuthorHouse   2/27/2007

ISBN: 978-1-4259-8345-1 (sc)
ISBN: 978-1-4259-9073-2 (hc)

Library of Congress Control Number: 2007900148

Printed in the United States of America
Bloomington, Indiana

This book is printed on acid-free paper.

Cover Photos:
Top: The Bund, Shanghai, China
Bottom Left: Mama in a kimono circa 1928
Bottom Middle: Food line in a refugee camp in the Philippines
Bottom Right: Me and Toshiko age 2

In Memoriam

To my beloved and dearest Mama, whose courage, strength, and unconditional love have been a shining beacon throughout my life.
To all the Russian émigrés who had to flee their homeland at the onset of Communism, for their indomitable spirit.

Dedication

I dedicate this book to my son, Nick, and his descendants. Be proud of your Russian heritage!

Acknowledgments

Many thanks to Mary Lindsay, who had faith in my story and strongly encouraged me to embark on this project. Although she is no longer with us, I hope she is looking down from above with her gentle smile.

I am grateful to Father Valery Lukianov for his kind advice and his permission to use the photo of the Russian Cathedral in Shanghai.

Kenji Harahata has my deepest gratitude for helping obtain a great deal of information about Kagoshima, and for his interest in my story.

My daughter-in-law, Susan, processed some very old photos for me—many thanks.

And, my husband, Nicolas, spent many hours assisting me in this venture. Merci beaucoup!

Hello Golden Gate
Goodbye Russia

Contents

Foreword		xiii
Chapter 1:	Leaving the Motherland	1
Chapter 2:	Harbin, China	31
Chapter 3:	Kobe, Kiushu, and Kagoshima	43
Chapter 4:	Olga Arrives	61
Chapter 5:	Our Life in Japan	83
Chapter 6:	Being Stateless	101
Chapter 7:	Shanghai	115
Chapter 8:	War in Shanghai	143
Chapter 9:	After the War	171
Chapter 10:	Shanghai at Limbo	179
Chapter 11:	The Philippines and Beyond	205
Epilogue		227
Japan Revisited		229
Recipes		237

Foreword

Dear Reader,

The stories I would like to share with you were told to me by my mother, and of course, captured through my own eyes. I have created dialogues to bring these stories to life, because it's impossible to know exactly what was said in every situation. However, given how vivid my mother's memory was in recounting our family's history, I'm confident that I have accurately reflected the words and emotions that were exchanged in the contexts of their times.

This is not a book on the history of Russia before and after the Revolution. Rather, it is about the individual people who were caught in the web of Communism's rise in Russia and China. I have written about how they had to leave behind everything they owned and everything they cared for, fleeing into the unknown with courage, holding onto each other and a culture that was dear to them. They were never to return to their homeland, yet with optimism, they searched for the soil they could set their feet on and call a new motherland.

–Olga Valcoff

Chapter 1:
Leaving the Motherland

Life Before the Russian Revolution

Most history books would have you believe that pre-revolutionary Russia was all darkness and misery, but I believe that isn't true. Yes, there were the merciless landlords, and the overworked working class; there were the aristocrats who had everything, and the peasants who had very little. But you could find those conditions in most countries in the world back then—and now, too, unfortunately.

In the 1800s, Russia started to develop a middle class who strove to achieve better lives and valued good education. Many educational institutions were established during this time in Moscow, St. Petersburg, the Urals, and other parts of the country. The people of the middle class were also ambitious in business, which led to the buildup of a merchant class. Known as the *Kuptsi*, they owned and operated Russia's small and medium-sized businesses, many of whom very successfully traded goods with foreign nations.

Several of Russia's most well-known industries began to emerge around that time as well. Coal and precious-stone mining became bigger businesses than they had previously been. Lumber also developed into a major industry, along with many lumber-related enterprises such as furniture-making, paper manufacturing, printing, and construction. Textiles, which had always been a staple of Russian culture, grew even more around this time—linens, silk, tapestries, brocades, laces—in addition to furs, which were well known for their high quality and were exported all over the world.

Across all classes, the arts flourished—composers, dancers, writers, and the theatre—much more than just the Dostoyevsky, Tolstoy, and Tchaikovsky the rest of the world knew. Reading was a favorite pastime, especially in remote areas, where a good book helped to pass the long winter days and nights.

The church was extremely pervasive across all facets of Russian culture. The church's rules and rituals were an integral part of most Russians' emotional lives, regardless of class, wealth, or political beliefs. Each family had their icons of the Virgin Mary, Jesus, and guardian saints displayed in a dominant area of each room—referred to as "the beautiful corner"—to protect the household. Entire communities came out for *maslenitsa*, the carnival-like celebratory week prior to Lent, then somberly observed the Lenten period with hard work, fasting, and daily church services. Easter was the most important holiday of all; after a midnight mass celebrating the resurrection of Christ, the festivities of the holiday often lasted for days that were filled with much drinking and eating.

As with all good things, this age of growth and prosperity did not last. 1905 brought Tsar Nicholas II's botched involvement in the Russo-Japanese War and a stirring feeling of dissension among the Russian people. This attitude fomented as Nicholas' reign became more incompetent and chaotic; by 1917, some Russians became disillusioned, and incited by Leninist Bolsheviks, they revolted. The Bolsheviks, to identify their movement, picked up the red banner and called themselves "The Reds." To oppose them, those who continued to support the old Tsarist regime identified themselves as "The Whites" or "The White Russians." This fact denotes a political distinction, not a geographical or racial one.

The fire of revolution began burning in St. Petersburg and the Moscow corridor, and then it spread throughout the nation with incredible speed. Fierce fighting occurred in cities and villages. As the Bolsheviks prevailed, the tsar's government toppled, and he and his family were brutally assassinated. The old ways of life were shattered and demolished.

All this happened within the period of only about two years. Properties and commercial entities were confiscated and redistributed by the new government, and private enterprises were completely shut down. Religion was abolished, and it was declared illegal to worship. Thousands of churches were either razed or burned down, or they were turned into warehouses and ransacked for valuables, as many icons traditionally were decorated with precious metals and jewels.

Everyone panicked, from the merchants and business owners to the middle and upper classes. Fear spread among the social strata as assassinations and lootings grew rampant. People who were not aligned with the revolutionary segment of the population were piled into vans and trucks and paraded down the streets; they were then carted off to an area that had been designated for executions, and they were shot to death. This happened to my husband's grandfather, who was a police official when the Bolsheviks took over. He was forced into a truck with a large group of men and taken away; his daughter ran after him, knowing that he was about to be killed, but of course, she was not allowed to get too close to where the murder would take place.

When trucks loaded with dead bodies began coming back out, the daughter ran from one to another, looking for her father. There were piles of men on each truck, and some were still alive. There were young boys who looked to be near death's door, holding out their hands to her and crying, "Help me, help me!" She went to each wagon as it passed by, but she never found her father.

Blood flowed profusely during the Russian Revolution. People were leaving everything behind and fleeing in any direction possible, but usually west to Europe and east to Asia, especially China. The diaspora of refugees climbed to over a million people.

This was the world of my grandparents, the Klukins and the Shlyapins, two very different families who ultimately ended up in the same place together.

The Klukins

Vassily Klukin, my mother's father, was born into a family of poor farmers in 1873. A robust and energetic boy, Vassily eagerly pursued his own education and learned subjects such as grammar and arithmetic from his brother, who was three years his senior and attended school. Reading was the favorite pastime of both boys, and on cold nights, they would huddle around the big kitchen stove, reading books and newspapers and daydreaming about exciting places they thought they would never get to see.

The boys enjoyed watching the twice-weekly trains come into the local station, where the conductors would even let them board the fiery steam engines on occasion. One day, while his brother was off at school, Vassily ran to greet one of the trains alone; when it came in with all its usual thunderous glory, a man wearing a uniform debarked. He tacked a poster to the station's billboard advertising the Imperial Navy's need for boys of thirteen years or older to become deckhands. Vassily's mind immediately snapped to all the stories he had read about adventures at sea, and he knew that he must find a way to go.

At dinner that evening, Vassily approached his father, Kapiton, about the situation. "Nyet, Nyet, NYET!" said his father, slamming down his spoon. "It is out of the question! I need your help here, with the farm and with chores. Gallivanting around the world is not for you!"

Poor Vassily's dreams were shattered. For the next several days, he sulked quietly, but his mother, Anna, recognized his disappointment. Though it would be sad for her to part with her son, she used all her persuasive skills to convince Kapiton to say yes.

"Can't you see that our son is miserable?" she asked her husband. "He is slow about his work, he doesn't want to eat, and he doesn't even read his books! All he wants is to join the Navy. There are worse things for a boy to wish for, don't you think?"

"I think that he should stop dreaming and pay more attention to his chores," Kapiton said gruffly.

"But don't you want him to have a good life?" Anna asked. "A better life than we have here on the farm?"

"There is nothing wrong with the life we have!" Kapiton objected.

"No, no, of course not," Anna conceded. "But Vassily has a chance to see the world—a chance he may never have again! Please, my dear, just think about it."

Kapiton was softened by his wife's demeanor, as he usually was, and in the end, he agreed to let his son join the Navy. The decision was a difficult one, and this fact was not at all lost on Vassily, who thanked his parents profusely and redoubled his efforts to be helpful around the house and farm for the next few months.

When spring finally arrived, Vassily packed a bag with a few belongings and bid his parents farewell. His mother was in tears, and his father was stoic. Vassily, however, could barely contain his excitement as he hugged them both, promised to write them letters, and then set off on what he was sure would be the journey of his life.

Vassily traveled across Siberia to board the Imperial Navy ship in Vladivostok, a port on the Pacific Ocean. Having grown up in landlocked country, he had never seen or smelled the ocean, and he immediately loved its briny scent and its rolling, cresting waves. The ship he was to board was larger than anything he had seen in his life, and it was bustling with sailors—loading cargo and supplies, laughing and joking, enjoying their last few minutes on shore before they boarded the boat and set out for their next long voyage.

Once they set sail, Vassily easily adjusted to his new surroundings and enthusiastically set about completing any task he was given. He was the youngest of five cabin boys, and because he quickly adapted to his assigned chores—scrubbing decks, cleaning toilets, kitchen duties—he was soon appointed to a young lieutenant, a count from St. Petersburg. The lieutenant liked his new assistant's cheerful, energetic personality and was astounded when he learned that Vassily could read and knew some math. He offered to tutor Vassily further in these subjects, and Vassily gladly accepted. During his eight years at sea, he took correspondence courses and earned the equivalent of a high school diploma; even more remarkably, he also received a fully accredited degree in civil engineering in the same way.

During his time with the Imperial Navy, Vassily circled the world twice by ship, even docking in Philadelphia at one point. When his seafaring career ended in 1894, he put all his knowledge to use as a builder of bridges and public buildings. By the time he was in his early 30s, he had become a wealthy, well-respected businessman, owning several brick factories and building roads and bridges in Lisva, a community in the Ural Mountains.

It was around that time that he met my grandmother, Pelaghia, who had been born and raised in Lisva. She was one of five children, though there were many cousins, uncles, and aunts who lived on the same street. They were a close-knit family of affluent merchants.

Lisva, Russia, my mother's birthplace c., 1905.

From an early age, Pelaghia was a happy girl with a pleasant personality. She went to a nearby girls' school and was educated properly. She was quite skilled in embroidery; just as many Russian girls at that time, she avidly pursued this talent. She also sang well and played piano.

Pelaghia was rather shy, but she happily entertained at parties and family gatherings, which were frequent at her home. On Sundays, after a long church service, it was traditional for people to gather at each other's houses for a hearty meal. Afterward, they would relax together in the parlor and play card games, tell jokes and gossip, and play music and sing. These times spent together with loved ones and friends were especially pleasant during the long, cold winters in the Urals.

Summers were also very enjoyable for young girls, however. When the weather was warm, one of their favorite activities was to go into the forest to gather mushrooms and berries, which grew in abundance. The older women then spent many hours making jams and marinating the mushrooms that the girls and young women had gathered. In addition, they pickled cucumbers and other vegetables to be stored for the next long winter.

Often, on Sunday evenings, the people of Lisva would gather outdoors to play music, sing, and folk-dance. At one of these gatherings, Pelaghia met a newly arrived neighbor, a wealthy young engineer named Vassily Klukin. The two took a liking to each other immediately, and before the night was through, Vassily had asked Pelaghia's parents if he could visit them and get to know their daughter. They said yes; he visited frequently, and so they fell in love. Their wedding took place in the spring of 1901, when Pelaghia was 17 years old.

*Grandfather Vassily, Grandmother Pelaghia
and her father Yakov Tooef.*

Pelaghia was a natural caregiver and homemaker; she was an excellent cook, and after her marriage, she kept her cellar stocked with fish, game, mushrooms, and fruit preserves that she made herself. Their relatives and friends often came to dinner, especially on Sundays, when elaborate meals of roasted meats, salmon or mushroom pies, caviar, rich butter and sour cream, and sweet cakes were served after the church services.

One of Pelaghia's favorite stories to tell involved herself and her cousin going for a walk in a park one summer afternoon. They were young women in their mid-20s, and they dressed up in their best, starched, white frocks for the outing. While strolling by a river, they saw a vendor selling fruits and vegetables, so they stopped to see what the man had to offer.

"Oh, Pelaghia," said the cousin, picking up an unfamiliar piece of fruit. "Look at this—it must be a new variety of apple!"

Pelaghia picked one up as well. It was red and slightly soft; it looked like an apple, but not like any she had ever seen. She smiled at her cousin. "Let's try them!" she said, taking a bit of money out of her purse and handing it to the vendor.

Eager to partake of these mysterious fruits, the women immediately bit into them, anticipating a taste that was familiar but perhaps different and better. However, they did not find the crisp, juicy sweetness they were expecting.

"Oh!" Pelaghia cried out as thick juice and tiny seeds gushed out of the fruit and ran in red stains down the front of her white, linen dress. She looked at her cousin, who was staring at her own dress speechlessly; the pristine fabric of her frock was totally ruined as well. Angered by this unanticipated turn of events, the two women threw their "apples" onto the ground and marched right back home to try to wash the stains out of their garments.

Though she did not see any humor in the situation at the time, later on, whenever Pelaghia recounted this story for her family and friends, she always laughed. "It was a long time," she would say, "before we appreciated ripe tomatoes!"

Pelaghia and Vassily lived on a popular main street in the town of Lisva. Vassily built a beautiful house for his family, full of modern conveniences—running water, electricity, even two bathrooms with flushing toilets. The house was designed for comfort against the cold winters in the Ural Mountains, with its thick walls, double-paned windows, many stoves, and front doors made of heavy oak. They had horses and carriages to get around town and three servants who lived in the house to help with cooking and cleaning. They had two daughters: Faina, my mother, born in 1903, and Nina, who arrived in 1905. Faina was artistic from an early age, always sketching and adorning her dresses with embroidery of her own design. Nina preferred racing around town on horseback. Both girls attended school, a privilege they appreciated so much that they never missed a class, even on the coldest of days.

"Fanya! Ninochka!" my grandmother would call to her daughters as she rushed up the stairs. "Do not plan to walk to school today. It's started snowing early, and it will be too cold for you dear girls to walk down the hill to your school. Mitya will drive you as soon as he has the horses ready. I can't believe we have a snowstorm and it's only early October!"

Nina jumped from window to window in her bedroom, watching the snowflakes fall. "Mama," she asked, "why don't we have a motor coach?"

*Aunt Nina age 5, Grandmother, mama age 7 and 2 cousins.
Grandmother is wearing a heart shaped locket,
which I have and treasure greatly.*

Pelaghia tried to put a white fur bonnet on Nina's head. It was lovely, with red ribbons to tie under her chin; Vassily had brought it for her from Moscow. "Because Lisva doesn't have a benzene station yet," she told her restless daughter. "Maybe soon! Then Papa will buy a motor coach for us. Please, Nina, don't wiggle so much! Look at Faina, she's already in her coat and has her books. Fanichka," Pelaghia said, turning to her eldest daughter, "you look very pretty this morning."

"Mitya's ready!" Nina announced, bounding away from the windows and out of the room. The girls ran together down the spiral staircase, laughing as they dashed out into the swirling snow and chilling wind, where their carriage driver awaited them.

Inside the house, Pelaghia leaned on the heavy, ornately carved doors to close them, and then she went to the great Victorian-style double windows of the parlor. She waved to her beloved daughters from behind the magnificent lace curtains that Vassily had brought her two years earlier from St. Petersburg. He went there often for business—and to Moscow and Perm as well—and always came back with beautiful gifts for her and the girls.

Vassily's prosperity continued over the years; his daughters grew into exceptional girls, and his relationship with his wife never lost the ardor of its first days. He had wealth, a beautiful home, and the respect of all who knew him—but he never forgot where he came from. Somewhere inside himself, he was still the poor farmer's boy who fought for every *kopek* he earned. He never forgot those early days of his life, so when he saw someone in a similar situation, he always wanted to help if he could.

This is how my grandfather came to know Alyosha. As my mother told the story, she was never quite sure where Alyosha had come from, or how the 10-year-old boy had come to meet Vassily, but she knew that he had been battered and abandoned by his family. Vassily brought him home one evening, and he stayed for five years. Vassily and Pelaghia cared for Alyosha as if he were their own son, even sending him to school alongside their daughters. He was smart, friendly, and full of humility for the help he received from the Klukin family. Then one day, just as suddenly as he had arrived, he was gone: an older cousin came to the house and took him away. My mother, Faina, was puzzled and sad; Vassily was heartbroken. He did not hear from Alyosha again for a long time.

The Russian Revolution Begins

The Bolsheviks—also known as the Communists—seized power in Russia in 1917, during the Russian Revolution. By 1919, they were going after business people and landowners throughout the country. Though in his personal life my grandfather was a quiet man with no political affiliations, he was targeted by the Communists because he was a landlord and an influential figure in his community. For no reasons other than those, he was arrested, jailed, and sentenced to death. There was no trial, no jury—just the Communists' belief that he was wealthy and important, and therefore too dangerous to let live.

Vassily spent two long weeks in jail. He had a small cell to himself; the other nearby cells were filled with his fellow merchants, men he recognized as business owners and landlords from Lisva. Two weeks he spent in silence, for the guards who roamed the jail did not allow any talking between prisoners. He prayed for his family, hoping that they would go on without him, that they would have the strength to survive.

On the 14th night of his imprisonment, a young man came into his cell. He wore the uniform of the Red Army, and Vassily thought that the time had come for him to be taken away, led to his death. But the boy—for the revolutionary soldier really was no more than a boy, in his early 20s at the most—pulled Vassily roughly to the rear of the cell, where no one could hear them speak.

"Mr. Klukin. It's me—Alyosha," the soldier told him. My grandfather lifted the brim of the young man's hat and looked into his eyes. He needed only one glance to tell him that this was indeed the peasant boy he had taken into his home years ago.

"Alyosha," said Vassily, moving to hug the young man, then realizing he had better not. He backed up against the wall again. "How did you get in here?"

"I'm in the Red Army," said Alyosha. "I saw you come into the jail a few days ago and I know that your execution is to take place tomorrow morning. I have been to see your family, Mr. Klukin—"

Vassily started at this. "Are they alright?" he asked feverishly. "My daughters, my wife, are they safe?"

Alyosha nodded, looking out the cell door and motioning to Vassily to keep his voice down. "Yes, they're fine, but listen to me. We can't waste any time. You have to get out of here—your family is packed and anxious to leave with you. I'm going to help you escape and join them tonight."

"Packed? Leave? To where?" Vassily was at once thrilled, of course, at the prospect of escaping his execution and being with his family again, but where were they expected to go?

"On the train, Vassily. The Trans-Siberian Railroad. It will take you to Harbin, a Russian settlement in China. It will be your family's only hope of survival." Alyosha straightened his hat and stood up straight. "I will be back tonight," he told Vassily. "I promise you."

Alyosha rushed out of the cell, and it was hours before he returned. Vassily heard him talking with the guard who was stationed at the end of the corridor. The two soldiers laughed and joked for a while— telling stories about the success of the revolution, the future, and of course, much about girls. Eventually, the conversation began to drift off, and then, there was no more talking. Alyosha came over to Vassily's cell.

"He's an old friend," he told Vassily, looking back toward the guard's station and smirking. "Likes to drink vodka but has no tolerance. He won't be bothering anyone here for a few hours."

Alyosha unlocked Vassily's cell door again, but this time, instead of coming in, he grabbed Vassily's arm and pulled him out—roughly, as though he were escorting a prisoner. Vassily understood that this was how it must look for him to successfully escape, though leaving the jail was easier than he had thought it would be—in Alyosha's custody, nobody questioned where they were going. Vassily was amazed by the authority his long-lost "son" now commanded.

Just as Alyosha had said, Pelaghia, Faina, and Nina were waiting at the train station at midnight. They had with them half a dozen suitcases and a couple of trunks filled with clothes, silver, and china. Their initial reunion with Vassily was happy but brief; they had a long journey ahead of them with plenty of time to talk things through. After they all said their tearful, thankful goodbyes to Alyosha, they boarded the train and left Lisva forever.

The Shlyapins

Nicolai Shlyapin, my paternal grandfather, was an accountant in Kizel, a town in the Ural Mountains of Russia. My grandmother, Paraskeva, was a housewife. They lived in a large apartment in the city and led a normal, quiet life. They were not rich or important enough to be harassed by the Communists, and would have lived out the rest of their lives in Kizel had it not been for an extraordinary set of circumstances involving the White Army and their only child, my father.

Alexandre Shlyapin, who went by the nickname Shura, was born in 1900. A handsome boy with dark hair and a lean figure, he was an only child after his sister died in infancy. When he was 17 years old, after only one year of studying engineering, he was drafted into the military division of Admiral Alexander Kolchak, who led the counterrevolutionary White Army.

Left: my father, age 10, Kizel, Russia.

Right: my paternal grandparents c. 1900

In 1918, China, Japan, the Bolshevik government, and Siberia's provisional Russian government were locked in a bitter struggle for control of Russian land in Manchuria. At the time, Kolchak was visiting locations in Manchuria and setting up anti-Bolshevik bases that increased the reach of the White movement, especially into Siberia. In this way, Kolchak and the Whites hoped to stop the spread of Communism from Moscow outward.

The idea of keeping Communism away from the Asian continent appealed greatly to the Russians who were already living in various areas of Manchuria. However, it was also attractive to the Chinese and Japanese governments; spurred on by Kolchak's plans, they signed an agreement that bound them together against their common enemy. Japan found this opportunity to perhaps stop Soviet Russia's encroachment upon Asia to be particularly beneficial to their own imperial plans.

Admiral Kolchak, however, refused any negotiations that the Japanese offered in support of his war on Communism. He would not for any price give up the territories that belonged to Russia—not even for much-needed military or financial assistance. Instead, Kolchak paid for his army's supplies from the Russian imperial reserve, which the Whites had seized in Kazan in August of 1918.

Kolchak's lack of cooperation did not sit well with the Entente nations—Soviet Russia, France, and the United Kingdom—who had their own separate agreements with Japan. They were, on the whole, more interested in money and land than in the ideals of the White Army, and when Kolchak was arrested and detained by the Soviets, Japan refused him any help. Kolchak was executed on February 7, 1920, by the Revolutionary Military Committee, but his White movement continued to spread across Siberia and into the east.

During this time of turmoil, the Red Army took advantage of Kolchak's disorganized forces and drove them back across the Ural Mountains, into Manchuria. When Nicolai and Paraskeva learned of this retreat, they knew that their son would never return to Russia, so they did the only thing they could: they went to look for him. Packing only the necessities—clothing, some food, and a few small, treasured possessions—they left Kizel, unsure of what hardships lay before them, or if they would ever return.

The Shlyapins rode a cattle train halfway through Siberia; later, in November, they were able to transfer to a passenger train en route to Harbin, the Russian settlement in Manchuria where many who fled the Communists ended up. With little available food and rampant infectious diseases, many of their fellow passengers died aboard the train, which stopped at intervals to dump the bodies of these unfortunate souls. They were left by the side of the tracks in piles, with no proper prayers or ceremonies to commemorate their passing.

After they had been riding this train for some time, Nicolai began feeling ill. Though he tried to hide it from Paraskeva, eventually that became impossible; he had contracted typhoid fever, and once it took hold of his body, he swiftly deteriorated and died. Paraskeva, having seen what had been done with other people who had passed away, demanded that her husband be buried.

"I am sorry," the train official told her as the train began to slow, "but we have neither the time nor the resources to accommodate your request. Your husband will be disposed of in the same manner as the others who are sadly deceased."

"Sadly deceased!" Paraskeva exclaimed incredulously. "What do you know about sadness? You push the bodies of these human beings out the door and into the snow as if they were sacks of garbage. My husband is not a sack of garbage. He *will* receive a proper burial!"

"Ma'am, please calm down," said the official, reaching to put a hand on her shoulder, but he was too late. Paraskeva had already marched past him, grabbed a shovel from a pile of tools that lay in the corner of the car, and swung open the train's door. It had just come to a complete stop; everything outside was silent except for the wind. Paraskeva jumped out, sinking knee-deep in snow, and turned back to the official.

"Bring my husband's body out here," she told him loudly, firmly. "Bring him to me. I will bury him."

The official shook his head. He tried to sound more forceful as he told her again, "We do not have the time for a burial. Get back on the train now. We'll be leaving again in a few minutes."

Paraskeva stood firm, shovel in hand. "Bring him here," she said slowly. "Then you can leave. I will bury him myself and wait for the next train."

The official was clearly taken aback. He straightened up, worry apparent in his eyes. "The next train might not come for two or three days, ma'am," he told her a bit more gently. "It's the dead of winter. You will not survive. Please, come back inside the train."

Paraskeva met the official's eyes and stood her ground in silence. After a few moments, the official walked back into the train car, out of Paraskeva's sight. *I cannot leave*, she told herself. *I cannot leave Nicolai behind*. She took a deep breath and waited, though she did not know quite what she was waiting for.

In a short while, the official returned, and he was not alone. Several men were with him, and they all had shovels. Between them, they carried the body of Nicolai Shlyapin. With some effort, they climbed down from the train and laid Nicolai on the snow, next to Paraskeva. One of the men took the shovel from her and began to dig.

"Thank you," Paraskeva whispered, tears freezing in her eyes as she looked back up at the official, still on the train. The man nodded at her in return, and then retreated into the train.

It took the gravediggers some time to accomplish their task, grunting as they sliced through a foot of snow and the layers of frozen ground beneath it. As they worked, Paraskeva knelt beside Nicolai, praying for him and saying her last goodbye.

Eventually, the crude grave was done, and at that point, to Paraskeva's surprise and relief, a priest stepped out of the train. He stood beside Paraskeva as her husband's body was placed in the cold earth. The priest then stood over Nicolai and administered the last rites to an accompanying chorus of howling winds and teeming snow.

Paraskeva was 40 years old and alone. She continued her journey by train, finding comfort in the companionship of her fellow passengers. Many of them, being from similar backgrounds, were greatly sympathetic to her situation and were glad to give any advice they could on how she might best be able to find her son once she reached Harbin.

"There are Russian newspapers in Harbin where you can place an advertisement!" one woman offered.

"I already have relatives there, and I will be glad to ask them if they know your son," said another.

"You can go to the refugee office," a man quietly told Paraskeva. "I am sure that they will be able to help you."

Nicolai's death, though a tragedy from which she would never fully recover, strengthened Paraskeva's resolve to see this quest to its completion. However, not long after she buried her husband, the train broke down in a small town, and everyone on it was forced to evacuate. After two weeks with no sign of another train, some passengers decided to continue on their way to Harbin, and Paraskeva bartered her gold bracelets for money to join this group. They were lucky enough to have horses and carriages to carry them; they faced rough terrain, animal attacks, lack of sanitation, and government rules at stations along the way. But they made it through Siberia, and through Mongolia, staying in villages and sleeping in huts. The band of 30 travelers did what they could to keep each others' spirits up, but they were beset by constant hunger, and many succumbed along the way. Only 14 of them made it to Harbin.

At some point during her journey, Paraskeva developed arthritis. As her condition worsened, the rigors of travel became difficult, as did simple, everyday tasks like brushing her hair. Paraskeva always had beautiful, long, black hair that was highlighted by luminous silver streaks as she had gotten older. When the pain in her hands prevented her from caring for her hair and keeping it styled as she wished, she simply cut it off. Her remaining hair styled into a short bob, she was at least comforted in knowing that she had less of a chance of getting lice while on her journey.

Paraskeva was in great pain when she arrived in Harbin. She had no possessions, save a small bundle with a few clothes and photos, but she had finally reached her destination, and the end of her quest was in sight. The first thing she did was to go to the refugee office and ask for help in finding her son. It was surprisingly easy—they were reunited within days, on October 23, 1925.

Shura, then 25 years old, did not even recognize his mother when he first saw her; her trials in getting to Harbin had aged her dramatically, and he missed her long, beautiful hair. Shura cried when he heard what his mother had endured to find him. To cheer her, he told her the good news that he was to be married within two days, to a lovely girl named Faina Klukin. Paraskeva was overjoyed at this, so happy that her son, whom she had once feared lost, was living a decent life and that she could now share it with him. Her long journey over, it seemed as though she was finally waking up from a horrible, five-year-long nightmare.

Chapter 2:
Harbin, China

The Rise of Harbin and the Stateless Russians

Typical building in Harbin, China.

By 1925, both sides of my family were safely in Harbin, Manchuria, a place where many refugees ended up during the turbulent years after their flight from Russia. Harbin was situated in an area of Manchuria that bordered Russia; culturally, it was somewhere in between—a blending of two ancient cultures that somehow managed to fit together.

Originally settled by Russian employees and builders of the Chinese Far East Railway in 1897, Harbin had grown from a sleepy fishing village into a large Russian city at the turn of the century. The railway connected China to the Russian Far East and was an offshoot of the Trans-Siberian Railway, the most reliable method of transportation at the time. Easily considered one of the industrial wonders of the world, its almost 6,000-mile stretch is still the longest continuous railway on Earth.

By the turn of the century, 50,000 Russians had settled and built Harbin. From 1918 on, during the exodus from the revolution, the number had swelled to 200,000 because of refugees seeking to escape the impending clutches of Russian Communism. The Trans-Siberian brought all kinds of Russians to Harbin: military leaders and officers, soldiers from the White Army and members of the White government, business entrepreneurs, and other people from all walks of life.

During the time when my grandparents and parents came to live in Harbin, the city had wide, tree-lined boulevards, streetcars, elegant European-style buildings, and many lovely parks and Russian churches. In addition, there were department stores, markets teeming with vendors and shoppers, bustling shops and restaurants full of lively customers, and most importantly, educational establishments. It was not home, and it was not the life to which they were accustomed, but it was a decent place for Russian middle-class citizens to begin to rebuild their lives.

Although by that time, they were no longer *citizens*. The Russian tsarist government ceased to exist when the Communists won the revolution. All who supported Communism and remained in Russia became Soviet citizens. Anyone else was cast aside with no country and no rights. This was what happened to Harbin's refugees: no longer under the protection of Russia's government, but not claimed by China's, they became stateless, people without a country or citizenship. They were called "The White Russians," and though they were wards of the Chinese government, that protection did not extend very far. They lived in China, but were not Chinese. They were Russian, yet they could not live in Russia.

Shura and Faina

In Russia, the Shlyapins and the Klukins had lived in neighboring towns, so it's not unreasonable to think that Faina and Shura may have casually met in the past. It wasn't until fate brought them both to Harbin, however, that the story of their life together began.

Having been on the run with Admiral Kolchak's army, Shura was not in great shape when he arrived in Harbin. His clothing was threadbare, and his shoes had holes, as did his short, fur overcoat and his faded hat. Days turned into weeks and then into months; he was without a job and had no permanent home. He had no family with him, no source of comfort. He was destitute in every sense of the word.

All that changed when Shura ran into Vassily Klukin as they passed each other on a street, one cold evening in 1921.

"Mr. Klukin, what a great surprise to see you!" Shura said excitedly to the older gentleman. "I'm Shura Shlyapin. Do you remember me?"

Vassily was startled; he looked up at the tall, lanky fellow. "My God! It is you. I hardly recognize you. How tall you've become! My goodness, how are you? When did you come here? Where do you live? Oh God, Shura, how skinny you are!"

"Oh, Mr. Klukin, I'm so happy to see you, sir!" Shura went on. "I've been here about two years, and I live in the army barracks. Unfortunately, I don't have any work, and it's very difficult for me. But I'm so glad to have been able to escape from Russia."

Vassily put his hands on Shura's shoulders. "It's good to see you," he said. It was obvious that the young man needed a good meal, a good bath, and some new clothing. "Shura, come home with me and have a big bowl of hot borscht, and we'll talk. Let me help you."

Shura smiled ear to ear, happy that his luck was going to turn, and to be reunited with people as fine as the Klukins. Perhaps there would be no more lonely days for him, piling one on top of another. He looked at Vassily's kind face. "Thank you, sir. I would greatly appreciate that."

Vassily took Shura home with him, where Pelaghia gave him a hot meal that he wolfed down and asked for seconds. After taking a long, hot bath, they set up a couch for him to sleep on.

Within a couple of days, Vassily found lodgings for Shura in a rooming house half a block down the street, and found him a job as a handyman in a warehouse, doing odd jobs but mostly shoveling coal several hours a day.

Shura visited the Klukins often, and he met Vassily's daughter, Faina. He was smitten with her lovely smile, peaches-and-cream complexion, sparkling hazel eyes, and curvaceous figure. Faina, too, fell in love with handsome Shura right away—he was such a gentleman, and she enjoyed talking with him for hours about anything and everything.

"Fanichka," Shura called her. "Would you like to go to a *maslenitsa* dinner party with me tonight at my friend Sasha's house? His wife, Panya, is an excellent cook, and Sasha plays an accordion and knows so many jokes. There'll be dancing, and singing—it'll be lots of fun. Come with me?"

Faina readily agreed; it was the first time Shura had ever invited her to a social evening with his friends, and she was very excited. When they arrived at Sasha Sloodkovsky's flat, it was just as Shura had described—full of the wonderful smells of Russian cooking, and the sounds of laughter and music. Panya greeted Faina like a long-lost sister, telling Faina as she fried *blinis* (thick, Russian pancakes—see recipe at the end of this book) all about how Sasha and Shura had been friends back in Kizel.

"It just goes to show," said Panya, "that saying is true: the more things change, the more they stay the same." She motioned toward Shura and Sasha with her wooden spoon, smiling at their antics in the next room. "Here we are in exile in a foreign land, and they're still singing and laughing like schoolboys."

Faina laughed, looking toward Shura in admiration. He was so full of life, despite the dire situations he had been through already.

Once Panya had finished cooking, everyone sat down at the table to talk, drink, and eat their *blinis* with smoked salmon, sturgeon, pickled herring, and red caviar, smothered with sour cream or melted butter. It was two days before Lent and time to remember the old Russian customs. After the opulent meal, Sasha picked up his accordion and began to entertain the guests with songs and jokes called *chastooshki*. Shura sat close to Faina, regaling her with stories of his exploits with Sasha, who was 10 years Shura's senior. He then listened intently as Faina, too, told stories about her own early life in Lisva. By the end of the night, they were holding hands.

Their love bloomed quickly, but they courted for three whole years before announcing their engagement. Grandfather—Vassily—was quite angry when Faina told him that she wanted to marry Shura; he wouldn't speak to them for a month. Papa was virtually penniless at that time, without a profession or stable employment. Grandfather envisioned a more prosperous match and a financially stable future for his beloved daughter. Finally, though, he relented, and gave the couple his blessing. They held their wedding on October 25, 1925, two days after Shura's mother had finally located him in Harbin, after her long journey.

The wedding was a quiet affair because times were obviously difficult for the once-affluent Klukin family. They married in a small church, attended by six ushers; as was Russian tradition, the ushers held crowns over the bride's and groom's heads throughout the ceremony, which lasted for over an hour. That was why there were three pairs of ushers—to trade off from time to time. Who could hold their arms in the air for an entire hour? Afterwards, Faina and Shura celebrated at a small restaurant with about 20 guests.

Faina and Shura—Mama and Papa, to me—both loved being social. Mama was sweet-tempered and very affectionate, an enthusiastic cook and homemaker; Papa was an elegant, well-read, articulate young man. He loved classical music and sang many opera arias, as he had a beautiful baritone. Papa was always the life of the party with his singing and joking. He was so entertaining that it was always easy for everyone to forget how cramped their small apartment was, and that they could only afford to serve simple cold cuts called *zakuski*, tea from a *samovar*, and a bit of vodka.

At the time of their marriage, Mama was employed at an elegant salon, doing embroidery on fashionable dresses and gowns. She received many compliments and bonuses for her fine work. Papa was working for a wealthy Italian man named Jacalo Sacho, who lived in an art deco house and entertained lavishly. Papa was Jacalo's greeter, gardener, and bookkeeper—a jack-of-all-trades, you might say. After a year of working at this rich man's estate, Papa lost his job because Jacalo went bankrupt. Suddenly forced to consider a new vocation, Papa and Mama went to their closest friends, Panya and Sasha, for advice about the situation. All four gathered around the *samovar* that night to talk things over.

"Oy, I think it's time to leave Harbin," said Papa with a sigh. He had been spending long hours trying to find work in Harbin, but to no avail. "There are so many new refugees every day," he said. "There just aren't enough jobs to go around. There's no future here."

Panya nodded. "I hate uprooting our family again," she said, looking toward Mama for support. "But I understand. It's a difficult time, in Russia and here in Harbin. Our stay here may be through."

"Well, how far are we willing to go?" inquired Sasha seriously. "You know, I worked in textiles in Russia, and I work as a tailor right now in a big store. I hear from my business friends about opportunities in Japan. They say the men there are very interested in Western attire, but have few suppliers. Shura, it's an easy market. Will you go with me to explore it?"

A silence fell over the room. They had come so far already—were they expected now to go even farther away from their motherland? How far would they have to go to find a place they could really call their home?

Chapter 3:
Kobe, Kiushu, and Kagoshima

Adjusting to a New Lifestyle in Japan

It did not take much to convince Shura that he could make a better life for his family in Japan. Within a week, he and Sasha left Harbin together to investigate the opportunities Sasha had heard about. Faina and Panya stayed behind in Harbin until their husbands found work and a place to live in Japan.

In the 1920s, Japanese men were beginning to be interested in wearing Western attire. Japanese women, however, continued to wear traditional kimonos and did not adopt Western styles until many years later. There seemed to be especially great interest in men's haberdashery in Japan's smaller cities and provinces, though any man looking to purchase any suits in the area ran into one big problem: there were only a few places to buy the clothing he wanted.

This was where Papa and Sasha came in. During their initial visit, they ended up in the city of Kobe, where they talked to many people and gathered a lot of information. Ultimately, they obtained a contract to represent an English textile company in provincial towns. Their actual work would involve taking fabric samples and fashion magazines to the potential customers, then taking orders for clothing based on these samples and pictures.

Once the contract was signed and steady work was secured, they sent for Mama and Panya. The four reunited in Kobe, and Mama and Papa settled into a Japanese-style house with thick *tatami* mats on the floors. Its rooms were partitioned by paper-lined *shoji* screens, and the furniture consisted of a chest of drawers, and a low table for eating, surrounded by thick cushions to sit on. They slept on the floor on a heavy futon mattress, which would be stored away during the day. The surroundings were very different and strange, but they were comfortable, although it was chilly in the winter.

As soon as they were settled in, the men went to work. They packed two suitcases full of textile samples and boarded a train headed for the southern province of Kiushu. Once there, they went from town to town on bicycles, soliciting clothing orders. They were a successful team because Sasha was a good businessman and Papa was a charming salesman. Papa loved Japan from the start, and he quickly learned to speak its language, which was fortunate for their business—the Japanese they dealt with did not speak Russian.

Sasha and Papa traveled for two or three weeks at a time, then went home to rest and see their families. Mama soon gave birth to a boy, Nicholas, and stayed with Panya and her son, George, who was eight years old. For the time being, life was calm and good, with modest prosperity both personally and professionally. After six months of success as traveling salesmen, Papa and Sasha had another idea.

"Why should we go to them when they could come to us?" Sasha asked as they all sat around the table, drinking tea from the *samovar*—the centerpiece, surely, of all their most important discussions and decisions. "There is a substantial demand for what we're selling. Don't you think that men would be willing to travel a little for the sake of a good suit?"

Papa smiled, his grin growing wider by the second as Sasha's unspoken proposal occurred to him. "A store, Sasha. What an excellent idea! Fanichka, what do you think?"

"If it means you'll be home more, I like it a lot," Mama replied.

Papa jumped up off the floor cushion and began pacing the small room. "We could hire tailors to make the clothes in our store. No more selling suits for bigger companies. We'll sell for ourselves! Sasha—what an excellent idea!"

My father's first store in Kagoshima.
Left to right: Papa, Uncle Volodya and a Japanese salesman.

The Business of Western Menswear

Papa and Sasha opened their first store in Kurume, in the province of Kiushu. Their wives joined them just as soon as the business and living arrangements were set up.

As Papa had envisioned, he and Sasha hired a crew of tailors as well as fabric cutters; in addition, they hired a local painter to adorn the front of their store with whimsical drawings and advertisements. And just as Sasha had predicted, the customers came from surrounding towns and provinces to buy their Western suits from the two already well-known sartorial salesmen.

One day, while Papa was tending the store, a professor from a nearby educational institution came in to make his first modern clothing purchase.

"Good afternoon, sir," Papa said in Japanese, which by then he spoke rather well. "What may I help you with today?"

The professor, looking a bit puzzled, gestured around the store. "I would like to purchase a suit," he said. "And your instructions on how to wear it."

Papa smiled. "Alright, then let's start at the beginning." He took a moment to size the gentleman up, and then he went to a shelf behind the counter and produced a truly Western invention: underwear. He handed the garment to the professor, who seemed awestruck by the button-front shorts. The concept and purpose were completely alien to him, partially because Japanese garments did not have anything resembling buttons; the kimonos were tied entirely by sashes and various strings. Seeing the man's confusion, Papa ushered him toward the back of the shop, where a thick curtain cordoned off the fitting area.

"You wear those underneath the trousers," Papa told the man, smiling and holding aside the curtain as the professor stepped inside. While he had a free minute, Papa dashed around the store, picking up shirts, ties, vests, socks—everything the professor would need to complete his new look. After a moment, though, the professor stuck his head out from behind the curtain.

"Excuse me," said the professor, beckoning my father toward him. "These—these things on the front of the—*underwear*. I do not know how to use them."

Papa smiled, knowing how uncomfortable it must have been for a Japanese man to ask for assistance with such a private matter. He stepped into the fitting area and professionally, deftly demonstrated how the buttons worked. The professor, being an intelligent man, understood quickly, and Papa went back to his clothes-gathering.

Over the next hour, Papa dressed this learned gentleman in full Western regalia: trousers, shirt, vest, jacket, necktie, socks, and lace-up shoes. By the time he got to the beautiful striped shirt, the professor was an old pro with buttons, though he did inquire as to whether the shirt should be buttoned in the back or the front. After giving a crash course in neckties and shoelaces, Papa stood back and regarded his work. The professor looked like a completely different man.

"Now," the professor announced, admiring himself in a full-length mirror, "I can go to Tokyo." He bowed in

Japanese style, paid his bill, and put in an order for two additional custom-made suits.

New Beginnings

After a year of being in business with Sasha, Papa began to get the urge to move on. Not because there was a problem, or any sort of bad blood between Sasha and himself. He was always on the lookout for something new and exciting to do, something to challenge him.

In 1928, Papa began to hear his customers talking about the city of Kagoshima. Lots of opportunities there, they said; many men, they said, who would like to buy quality clothing from a reputable vendor. These conversations put ideas in my father's head about striking out on his own and moving to Kagoshima to start his own store. So before long, he, Faina, and Nicholas were once again packed up and on the road.

Kagoshima was a picturesque city with beautiful parks and, to my parents' great happiness, one Russian Orthodox Church. Situated on Kagoshima Bay, its postcard-like background featured a great, active volcano, the Sakura-jima, from which plumes of smoke constantly emanated. The city was lush with greenery, with palm trees growing alongside pines. I call Kagoshima "the Naples of the Orient," an understandable comparison: both were southern port cities located on a bay, both known for their temperate climates with cool breezes from the bay, with a volcano in the background.

*Papa's elegant men's haberdashery.
Our apartment was on the second floor.*

My father opened an elegant men's salon in a modern building on a busy, central street with streetcars running along it. Many of his customers were important men—government and university officials among them—who still dressed in the traditional Japanese kimonos but were eager to "convert" to the Western style. Papa taught these men how to wear the Western attire, and because of his charming, diplomatic demeanor, his business became very successful. He eventually made good money and had a good credit line with his textile suppliers.

Papa, Mama, and Nicholas lived in an apartment above the shop. The apartment occupied two floors: on the first, there was a dining room, an extra room for tailors to work in, and a kitchen; upstairs was a large living room where Papa often played his prized Victrola, a large bedroom, and a glassed-in room where they kept their pet canary. The apartment's floors were plywood covered by *tatami* straw mats, so they adopted the Japanese custom of walking around the house barefoot or in slippers, to keep street dirt from soiling the mats. They put scatter rugs and Western furniture in the rooms to make it seem a little more like *their* home. Every day was a challenge and every step was a learning process.

Their street was one of a few paved, as it was a busy thorough-fare with the streetcars running along. It was in Tenmonkan district where many small shops and businesses lined both sides of the avenue. A men's hat shop, a barber, bus depot, orthopedist and a bakery were across from our place. A bank set in a beautiful garden and in a Japanese style building, a Japanese traditional furniture store, a music store and even a tavern were on our side of the street. Around the corner was a sushi shop and a Japanese bathhouse that my family frequented. Needless to say this area was a lively one where the residents were friendly and socialized with each other. They embraced the Shlyapins warmly after they settled in the neighborhood.

When my family moved to Kagoshima, only about a dozen Western families lived there. Mama and Papa made friends easily wherever they went, so they soon became close with the Moores, an American missionary family, as well as families from Germany and Portugal. Mama also formed a close friendship with Ilsa, a German gal who was married to a Japanese doctor. Their interracial marriage caused a big rift with his parents, who refused to accept a foreign wife into their family; the Japanese have a closed, homogeneous society. Later on, the couple had a boy about my age who became a big pal of mine. Mama told me that the boy's hair was brown and his mother dyed it black so he would be better accepted among his Japanese friends.

Mama and Papa made many Japanese friends, too; my mother liked Japanese people in general for their cleanliness, their sophisticated culture, their polite and dignified manners, and their delicious food. Though she did sometimes miss having many Russian companions, Mama adapted to her surroundings well and eventually formed a group for "ladies' tea" once a month with her one Russian friend plus an American, a German, and a Japanese woman. Imagine a diverse group of women sitting around a table, sipping black or green tea, eating European

My mother in a Kimono.

pastries and Japanese sweets, and conversing in Japanese, their common language. They formed a warm friendship that lasted many years.

Though my mother had friends while living in Kagoshima, she often found herself with a lot of time on her hands while Papa was tending to his business. In her boredom one day, she went and bought a Singer upright sewing machine with which she could practice her embroidery. She sketched baskets of flowers and transferred them onto linens, mostly table runners and tablecloths. She was quickly enamored with the hobby, and her talent was apparent; her friends admired her work greatly and were always happy to receive a beautifully embroidered runner as a gift. Much later, for my fifth birthday, Mama embroidered a dress for me—it was white chiffon, and she decorated it with the most lovely, delicate pink- and lilac-colored flowers, scattered all around the hem and on the short, puffy sleeves. I was so proud of that dress! Today, I still have several pieces of my mother's original embroidery, which have held up wonderfully over the years. I cherish them for their beauty; they are truly works of art, made by my mother's own hands.

My father c. 1930.

Before long, my grandmother, Paraskeva, came from Harbin to live with my family in Kagoshima. The rheumatism she had developed during her five-year trek from Russia to Harbin had by then overtaken most of her body, and she was in constant pain. My parents partitioned a bedroom for her in their first-floor dining room, with curtains around her bed made of summer kimono material, white with blue dots.

By 1933, Papa's business was flourishing, and Mama was pregnant with me, their second child. One lovely April day, just as Mama had gone downstairs to make Papa his lunch, a young Japanese girl came into the store.

"Good afternoon," she said to Mama and Papa meekly. They returned her greeting, though they were a little taken aback; teenage girls were not the average customer in Papa's store.

"My name is Chizuko," the girl went on, "and I need a job. I can do anything—mend clothing, clean, sweep floors—anything! Please, I just need to work!"

Papa and Mama looked at each other. What were they to make of this girl? "I don't know," Papa began. "You're very young—"

The girl began to cry. "Please!" she begged. "Please! I'm 16 years old. My stepparents are forcing me to marry a man who's old enough to be my father. I don't want to marry him! I'm so scared, I ran away. Please, I need a job to support myself. If I ask for work from Japanese people, they will be obligated to return me to my stepmother. That is why I came to you. I will be forever grateful." She looked down at her feet and continued to cry quietly.

My parents turned to each other again, this time with looks of worry. "Shura," Mama said softly. "I could use help around the house until the baby is born. I get tired easily now. Can't we help this poor girl?"

Papa nodded without a second thought. "Of course," he said, turning back toward Chizuko. "Stop crying," he told her. "You can stay. We need the extra help!" And that was how Chizuko became my parents' housekeeper—though in time, she was less an employee than an additional member of the family.

Father Ioan Takejiro Ooki, the Japanese Russian Orthodox priest who baptized me.

Two months later, our family again increased in number. I arrived on June 16, 1933, after a very difficult labor attended by a midwife at my parents' home. They were both thrilled to have a girl, though it's been said that I made Papa especially happy. The Japanese priest in Kagoshima's lone Russian Orthodox Church baptized me in a beautiful ceremony; several of my parents' Russian friends came to town just for the occasion. My start in life was joyous and full of love, two qualities that my family never lost, even during the difficult times to come.

Chapter 4: Olga Arrives

My Early Life

*Family protrait in front of our store.
Left to right: Mama, me, Papa, Grandmother and my brother.*

I was five years old before I realized I was not Japanese. At that time, we had family friends whose oldest son was drafted to be a pilot in the elite Japanese military forces. A banquet was planned in his honor, and I assumed that my parents and I would be invited.

The family's youngest son was one of my pals. When I mentioned the party to him, and told how excited I was to attend, he said to me, "Oh no, you cannot come. You are *gaijin*…a foreigner." I was stunned, but his proclamation truly opened my eyes. For the first time, I realized that my family and I were not like everybody else.

The government did not grant me citizenship, though I was born in Japan—no Caucasians were given that status at the time. All my friends were Japanese; we played the same games, dressed the same, and spoke the same language. I suppose I was not aware enough to realize that my blonde hair and blue eyes were different in appearance from the rest of the Japanese children.

Three friends, age 4, with a little brother.

One of the friends I remember from my early childhood, Kinuko-chan, lived in a house with a lovely garden and a fish pond, is an intergral part of my earliest memory. Our cat had killed our familiy's pet canary, a pretty bird that I adored, that I burried in Kinuko-chan's garden. I even made a cross for it's grave and sang a song at it's "funeral service". I was about three years old.

Kinuko-chan's parents owned the barber shop and were occupied most of the time at their establishment. They did not permit her to hang around the shop so she spent a great deal of time at our house. She and I became very close. Nevertheless we had our spats. I remember one occasion when I hit her with a toy shamisen, a Japanese mandolin. She brought the toy with her but refused to let me play. The tug-of-war ensued and I yanked the shamisen and hit her on the nose. I guess I didn't know my own strength because it was a hard hit, and she ended up with a nosebleed. My mother panicked when she saw what had happened, not because the girl had a minor injury but because some blood had dripped down onto her dress. She quickly washed and ironed the girl's clothes.

"Please, do not say anything to your mother," Mama told my friend as we walked her home. But as soon as we reached her house, her mother knew something had gone wrong. How did she know? Not because of our guilty looks, but because she could see that the girl's dress had been ironed—something that the Japanese generally did not do with casual children's clothing. The dress had to be ironed in order to dry it as there were no clothes dryers available at that time.

Another friend, Akie-chan came to play often. She was astounded to see such a "huge" bed, which was my parents' double-bed. The Japanese did not have beds. They slept on futons on the floor and put them away each morning. One day she and another friend Toshiko-chan and myself, decided to jump up and down on that bed, no doubt squeeling with glee. Unfortunately for us, mama walked in and lost all her composure! She pulled us off the bed and gave us "substantial" spanks and banished us to the living room. Our apartment became a favorite place to play "hide-n-seek" as the couches, large armchairs, drapes and of course that famous bed provided good places to hide. The Japanese homes, without much furniture, were not the places where the children could indulge themselves in this game.

That was a rare occurrence, though; I didn't often fight with my friends, and I was perfectly capable of getting into trouble all on my own. Once, when I was one and a half, I wandered outside Papa's store. For some reason, to my child's eyes, the streetcar tracks running in the middle of the street seemed like an excellent place to play. I went right over to them and sat myself down.

Mama, who was tidying our second-floor apartment, and Chizuko, who was busy in the kitchen, noticed a crowd gathering outside. They didn't think too much of it, but that was understandable—we lived on a busy street, and it was often full of people. They had no idea that I was the center of the crowd's attention.

As I sat on the tracks, two streetcars came toward me from opposite directions. If it hadn't been for the crowd's yelling, they might have run me over! Instead, they stopped yards apart, facing each other right outside Papa's store. Thank goodness for the streetcars' conscientious drivers; one of them even scooped me up and brought me back inside, where Papa, Mama, and Chizuko were all alarmed to hear what had gone on without their even knowing it.

Mama was very happy that she decided to hire Chizuko, as she had turned into a real gem. She quickly picked up our Western ways and learned how to cook Russian meals. She energetically ran our household, always smiling and chattering, always offering good advice. One day, while Mama was preparing Russian ground-meat patties called *katletki*, Chizuko asked, "Why do you use salt so much? Wouldn't it be better to use soy sauce instead?"

"Soy sauce!" Mama exclaimed. "Chizuko, I don't think that would taste very good with Russian food."

"Oh no, it would make the meat more moist and flavorful. Let's try it," Chizuko said good-naturedly, "and if I'm wrong, you will never have to take my advice again."

Mama did try making her *katletki* with a little soy sauce, and to her great surprise, Chizuko had been right. The meat came out wonderfully delicious! Mama happily assured Chizuko that she would heed any cooking advice she offered from then on, and thus was born a Japanese adaptation of a traditional Russian dish (see recipe at the end of this book).

Once, when I was four years old, Mama sent me down the street to buy some soy sauce. I had often gone on this errand with her as well as without her. In Japan, it was safe for a child of my age to go on such a task alone—or so we thought! This time, I was sent out by myself, and though I should have been back within 20 minutes, 40 minutes passed and I didn't return. My family went out to search for me, and before long, they found me: I had slipped on the muddy road and fallen into a square manhole. I had been yelling for help for about half an hour, but the traffic—the cars, bicycles, and people—were moving so fast around me that no one could hear my cries. Papa finally spotted me and pulled me out of the manhole, where I had been trapped up to my knees in muck, terrified, trembling, and crying my lungs out.

I remember that entire episode, even though I was very young. Another thing I remember from around that time was a great fire that started in the middle of the night, several blocks away from our home. It was so violent, and caused such an uproar—everyone was awake and out in the streets or watching from their windows, as my parents and I did. It was an entire street in flames, as the Japanese structures were made primarily of wood and paper *shojis* that easily could catch fire from one to the other.

"What a terrible thing," Mama said quietly to Papa. "The poor people who live on that street!"

Papa nodded his head solemnly. "They'll likely lose everything," he noted. After watching everyone scurrying around outside for a while, he added, "I hope the wind doesn't blow this way."

Mama looked at him; apparently, this thought had not yet occurred to her. "Shura," she said. "If it does, the fire will surely reach our building."

Papa nodded again. "I think we should have our bags ready, Fanichka," he said, and with that, Mama went and packed a few of our valuables and some clothing in two suitcases. If the fire threatened our home, we would be ready to evacuate.

I clearly remember pressing my little hands to the glass windowpanes, staring over the roofs of the houses, mesmerized by the raging flames. Fortunately, the wind shifted and the fire never came in our direction, but the sights and sensations of that horrifying night have never left my mind. To this day, I get shivers when I see a fire.

Aside from these occasionally jarring episodes, my family had a pleasant life in Kagoshima. Papa was successful and respected by many. Mama often said that the time in Kagoshima was the happiest time of her life; she especially loved the climate and the parks. Though my parents knew only basic Japanese, they communicated comfortably with the natives.

One August, my former nanny, Taka-san, invited me to visit her village on the outskirts of Kagoshima. This was during the O-bon festival, a Buddhist commemoration of departed souls. As part of the festival, there were parades in which people carried paper lanterns, each representing a loved one who was no longer with them. The parades wound their way to the river, where the lanterns were set on the water, symbolically releasing the departed souls.

As the lanterns floated down the river, children gathered on the banks to catch fireflies. They had contests to see who could catch the most, all the while singing a song called *Hotaru* that went something like, "Water there, firefly, not so good—water here sweet!"

Taka-san and I stayed in the country for several days enjoying the festival, watching parades, listening to the huge drums that were played in the parades, eating plenty of delicacies, laughing, and singing with other children. I have fond memories of this wonderful and idyllic time. I learned much later in my life what a serious tradition the O-bon festival was, and what an honor it was that Taka-san had taken me with her. It meant that she considered me part of her family.

Blending the Cultures of East and West

Russian culture was predominant in our household. It was a great pleasure for my parents to spend time with Panya and Sasha, who lived about a hundred miles away; they visited each other whenever possible and immersed themselves in all aspects of being Russian. They truly relished hanging onto their old culture and reminisced about life in Russia, the holidays, the food, and music. Sasha was usually enthusiastic about entertaining with his accordion and his songs.

My Aunt Nina, who still lived in Harbin, sent me Russian children's books. My parents read them to me, and began to teach me how to read and write in Russian. I loved the stories and fairy tales in those books, as well as their beautiful pictures.

"Mama, please read to me about *snegoorochka*," I would say, referring to a story about the snow maiden, one of my favorites.

"Yes, my sweet," Mama would say gently. "Sit down on the couch, I'll bring a cup of tea, and we'll read it together. Aunt Nina said that next time she will send you a children's magazine called *Lastochka—The Sparrow*."

I enjoyed the times my mother and I spent reading books together immensely. It seems the love of reading was firmly planted into my character at that time. But my reading was not limited to Russian print. Chizuko and other Japanese friends read Japanese books to me as well, and I greatly enjoyed those as well. Fairy tales and ghost stories had equally special places in my heart.

At home, Chizuko helped with the cooking, learning with great skill how to prepare our favorite Russian dishes. She sometimes surprised us with delicious Japanese meals, too.

Christmas pafeant at Miss Finley's Keiai Youchien School. I'm on the far right, sitting on the floor.

Mama still cooked most of the meals, and it was always a treat to taste her wonderful dishes, whether she had invented them herself or learned them from her mother and grandmother. She became enormously popular with our neighbors with her meat Pirojki, which were dough puffs filled with ground beef (and a dash of soya, of course) that were deep-fried. My little friends, and their parents, were often treated to these delicious buns.

Of course, when we went out to eat, we only had one cuisine to choose from, but we enjoyed visiting the many Japanese restaurants and teahouses in our neighborhood.

American influences entered my life when I was three. I began attending a preschool run by Miss Finley, an American missionary; it was a Christian-based institution, but only a few of the children were Christian Japanese. Needless to say, Miss Finley and I were the only Caucasians. She celebrated the Christmas traditions with all the students, producing a nativity pageant that was a highlight of every school year. Though she conducted all classes in Japanese, we did learn some English-language and American songs. She was wise enough to pick songs with lyrics that were easy for Japanese children to pronounce. Oh, the three years I spent in her care were lovely!

The rest of my American "education" came from the movies that Mama took me to see. They featured stars such as Shirley Temple, and Judy Garland in *Andy Hardy* films. I enjoyed MGM musicals as well, but my special favorites were Disney and other cartoons. American movies were very popular in Japan by this time, and Mama and Chizuko frequently visited the local movie houses. Chizuko especially loved the movies, as she enthusiastically embraced all that was Western.

*At Keiai Youchien School. Miss Finley is on the left;
I am perched on the top left corner*

Though it's a little less material in nature than nationalities and customs, you could say that I learned to appreciate classical music at an early age. Papa often relaxed by listening to classical music on his Victrola; occasionally I sat on his lap and listened too, enraptured by the music and the stories he told me about the great composers. He knew and enjoyed operas, and he could sing many arias in his beautiful baritone. He once went to Tokyo with Sasha to hear a performance by a very famous basso, Feodor Chaliapin, a Russian opera singer of international fame. This was a great event for Papa—one that he talked about for many years afterward. Unfortunately, Mama had to stay home to run the business in our store, which she enjoyed and did very efficiently.

Returning to Harbin, 1937

At the dinner table one evening, Mama appeared pensive. She looked up at Papa and said, "Shura, it's been three years since I saw my parents. I miss them very much! Don't you think I could go this summer to visit them and Nina? I'll take Olga along with me."

"Excellent idea!" replied Papa. "They'll all be delighted to see the two of you. Perhaps you'll be able to convince Nina to move to Japan, and leave that good-for-nothing man she lives with. He gives her nothing but grief and humiliation! It's time she left him. She could easily establish her dental practice in this country, especially in Tokyo or Kobe, where there are many Russians and Europeans." Turning to me, Papa added, "Your other grandma will be in seventh heaven to see you, and surely she'll spoil you with her cookies and cakes!"

"Oh, wow," I said. "We're going on a long trip. Hooray!" I yelled, jumping up and kissing everybody at the table.

Mama looked at me and sighed. "I'm certainly happy to go, except that I dread the sea voyage. You know I get terribly seasick, Shura. I hope there will be some nice people to help me with Olga."

"Don't worry, Mamochka," I said, hugging her. "I'll be a very good girl, I promise."

Mama began making plans and preparations for our journey. In early June, when the weather was warm enough in northern China, we took a train to the seaport of Shimonoseki and set sail to Pusan, Korea. The sea voyage was not as difficult as Mama had anticipated, and we arrived safely in Pusan, where we continued our trip to Harbin by train.

Once in Harbin, I was surprised to see so many Russians and to hear the Russian language everywhere. As soon as we arrived, Nina rushed toward us; she and Mama embraced each other, kissing and weeping profusely, united again in their profound love. Then Aunt Nina scooped me up in her arms, crying and laughing, and took out a big chocolate bar. I knew from that moment that I loved her forever!

From the station, we went directly to Aunt Nina's apartment. The height of the ceilings and the enormous windows amazed me. We stayed in Harbin nearly two weeks, during which time Mama rushed around visiting many old friends. She took me to her high school and introduced me to her old teachers. One Sunday we all went to the big cathedral, where I stood in astonishment—we stand throughout the service, as we do not have pews in Russian churches—looking at the magnificent frescoes that had been painted throughout the entire sanctuary. Another time, Aunt Nina took me to see Russian puppets, to my great delight.

Our stay in Harbin flew by, and when our time there was up, Nina accompanied us to my grandparents' house. This was a big change of scenery; they lived in a remote Chinese village about three hours by train from Harbin. There were no Russians living in the area, only Chinese people. A tall brick wall surrounded my grandparents' small cottage, and they had a small yard where my grandmother grew flowers and some vegetables. They had a barn with a cow and a couple of dozen chickens. When we arrived, we were greeted loudly by a bouncy German shepherd, who jumped on Nina and licked her face, wagging his tail and squealing with joy. My grandparents ran out to greet us with hugs and tears. Then, they ushered us into the house, which was full of delicious smells. The *samovar* was already set up, and in the true Russian tradition, we sat around the table, eating and talking until late that night.

Visiting maternal grandparents in China.
Left to right: Grandma, Mama, me and Aunt Nina.

Everything there was new to me. I frolicked around the yard, chasing chickens and playing with the dog. Each morning, I was amazed to watch Grandpa milk the cow, and I thoroughly enjoyed the glass of fresh, warm milk that it produced. I had never imagined just how milk came out of a cow, and the firsthand knowledge of it made me feel very grown up.

"Wow, Grandma," I said, "I'll tell my friends all about how milk is made. They won't believe me!"

"But your teachers will," Grandma told me wisely. "They will say that you're telling the truth! So tell your friends all about what you learned. Here, have some cookies!"

My memories of that lovely visit revolve around smells, it seems—smells of Grandma's cookies, and hay in the morning, but especially of the sweet, freshly cut grass after a quick summer rain.

Unfortunately, it all had to come to an end eventually. I wished to stay longer, but it was time to say goodbye and board a train again. Mama wept hysterically, clinging to her parents until Nina came to take us back to Harbin, where we had time only to change trains and head for Pusan again. Needless to say, the farewell with Nina was heart-wrenching.

The entire trip back was uneventful. My father greeted us at the Shimonoseki train station gleefully, and then life returned to its normal routine. I was loaded with many presents and proud of my journey.

Stricken With Asthma

In the fall of the same year, I became ill with diphtheria. I had a high fever that kept me in bed for several days. Today, our children are inoculated with DPT serum, which fortunately prevents them from getting this terrible disease.

After I recovered, I kept coughing and wheezing for a length of time, to my parents' consternation. My doctor eventually concluded that I had developed asthma as a result of having diphtheria. I became very susceptible to frequent colds, often resulting in asthma attacks that kept me in bed for several days at a time. Physical activity, such as running or jumping, became difficult making me gasp for air and wheezing, and not being able to fill my lungs with enough oxygen. My life changed. My illness affected my parents deeply, making them constantly worry about my health. My life had been greatly and adversely colored by this ailment.

Chapter 5:
Our Life in Japan

View of Kagoshima Bay with Japanese Military ships patrolling c. 1938.

Japan Prepares for War

Japan began invading other Asian nations as early as 1931 with the Mukden Incident, wherein their military blew up a portion of the South Manchuria Railway and blamed it on Chinese dissidents. Because of this, the Japanese government was able to move in and annex Manchuria, which is seen by some as the official beginning of the Second Sino-Japanese War. Over the next few years, Japan made its way down through northern China, occupying its land piece by piece until they reached and overtook Shanghai and Nanjing in 1937.

Those of us living in Japan at this time did not hear very much about any of this. Most knew that something was happening, but not the true extent of it; the only news sources were radio and papers, both of which were subject to regulation by the Japanese government. The only reports that ever came through—throughout this war and World War II—were about Japanese military victories.

My family, however, did not read the Japanese papers, and the regular radio stations were difficult to understand. Instead, Mama and Papa got their news from Russian newspapers and shortwave radio that picked up Russian and American transmissions, as well as from the many rumors that generally spread around between us Russian people. These were the sources that first brought us word of Hitler's expansion into Europe and Japan's forming an axis with the despotic German leader.

We were, however, eyewitnesses to one of Japan's wartime preparations: the building of an enormous naval base in Kagoshima Bay. Military airfields were being built on the city's outskirts. Many years later, we learned that these airfields were actually kamikaze bases; the planes that would eventually take off from their runways were really suicide bombers en route to meet their targets, the Allied forces in World War II.

As these structures rose around the city in which my family lived, the Japanese government decided that they no longer wanted foreigners in the vicinity of Kagoshima. Such economic pressures were put on non-Japanese merchants in the area that it became increasingly difficult to keep their businesses running, and it wasn't long before almost all the foreigners in Kagoshima were gone.

People Leave

Sasha, Panya, and their son George were living in Kurume at this time. When George graduated from the well-respected Canadian Academy high school in Kobe, he was accepted to the University of Washington in Seattle. His parents proudly saw him off on his trip to America.

Before long, Sasha and Panya decided that it was time for them to leave Japan as well; their situation in Kurume was not as difficult as ours was in Kagoshima, but it was certainly not easy as it had once been. Mostly, they missed their son, and they had heard that there were business opportunities to explore in America, so they decided to move to Seattle. They sold their business and rapidly made preparations for their departure.

Before embarking on their journey across the sea, Sasha and Panya made time to visit us in Kagoshima. They stayed for a few days, reliving old memories and talking about the future. They sat around the table, drinking tea from the *samovar* as well as a bit of vodka, and eating the Russian delicacies known as *zakuski*. Sasha played songs on his accordion, but his usual jokes were in short supply. This certainly was a sad time for Mama and Papa; they were losing their oldest, dearest friends. Who knew how long it would be before they were to see each other again—if ever?

When Sasha and Panya said farewell, there were of course many tears, though we all wished them well on their new venture. Shortly after, they left for the United States, fortified with optimism for their future.

Above: Farewell photo of my family and the Sloodvoskys before they left
Below: Aunt Panya, Mama and me at age 4 and a half.

But my family's loss did not end with Sasha and Panya's departure. A couple of months later, in February of 1939, we received an urgent telegram from Harbin. Papa took it from the deliveryman and opened it with hesitant fingers. His eyes quickly scanned the message.

"No…no!" he whispered, tears immediately welling in his eyes. "It can't be!" He shook his head as he reread the telegram, wishing that he had misunderstood it. But he had not: the message did inform him that Aunt Nina, Mama's sister, was dead. She had committed suicide! The telegram was from Aunt Nina's best friend in Harbin. Aunt Nina had passed away the previous night. She took her own life because of her love for the man she lived with for almost 10 years. He was married at the time Nina became involved with him. Then after all this time he left Nina for another woman, an 18 year old girl. It must have become unbearable for poor Nina and she despaired and committed suicide by taking poison.

How will I tell Faina? Papa thought, though he knew that telling her was exactly what he must do, right away. He told his manager to mind the store, and then heavily ascended the stairs to our apartment. Mama was in the dining room, setting the table for lunch, chatting with my grandmother as she worked. She stopped when Papa slowly entered the room.

"Shura," she said, "What is it? Are you all right? Are you hurt?" The look on his face—the tears in his eyes—Mama thought for a moment that he had somehow been injured.

"I'm fine, Fanichka," he said quietly, hanging his head.

"Olga!" Mama exclaimed. "Where is Olga? Olga!" she called.

I heard Mama calling me from the kitchen, where I was watching Chizuko prepare our midday meal. I ran into the dining room. "Mama!" I said as I bound through the door. I stopped short when I saw Papa, so distraught. "Papa?" I asked.

He managed a weak smile. "I'm fine, Olinka," he said to me. "Go on and help Chizuko." He waved me back into the kitchen. I have never seen my parents look so terribly distraught. I realized that something incomprehensibly terrible has happened. I quietly sat in the kitchen as Chizuko went about her chores looking puzzled and worried as to what was happening in the dining-room.

Mama watched me disappear back through the door, then turned to Papa expectantly. He did not know what to do, so he just held the telegram out in front of him.

"What is it?" Mama asked.

"A telegram," said Papa. He took a deep breath. "Oh, Fanichka, Nina has died!"

From the kitchen, I heard my mother scream and the crashing of the stack of plates she had been holding as they hit the floor. I jumped up from my chair, but Chizuko put her hand on my shoulder and sat me back down. She too looked concerned, though she did not know what was going on in the next room.

"How?" Mama cried. "Oh, Nina, what happened to her?"

"She took poison," Papa told her, pulling out a chair for Mama. She sank down onto it, holding her head in her hands, her tears unstoppable.

"Oh, my sister," she sobbed. "It can't be! She promised us that she would come to Japan. How could she leave us this way? Oh my God, oh my God!"

Papa stood next to Mama's chair and embraced her, though he knew the situation was inconsolable. "It was that man she lived with, Fanichka," he said. "He drove her to it. She should have left him long ago!"

"Oh, poor Nina. What horror!" Grandma exclaimed, pressing her handkerchief to her eyes.

Mama cried loudly. In the kitchen, I decided that I couldn't take just listening to her any longer, and I dashed past Chizuko into the dining room. I ran up to Mama; I had never seen her so devastated. And Papa—Papa was crying, too! This was something that I had never seen, and it upset me more than anything. It was the first time I saw Papa weep.

"Oy, oy, Olinka," Mama said, hugging me as she cried. Papa collapsed onto a chair and covered his face with his hands. They were both in a state of shock.

Suddenly, Mama raised her head and opened her eyes wide. "Oh no!" she exclaimed. "My poor parents!" Fresh tears came to her eyes. "They don't have a telephone. I have no way to console them."

Papa put a hand on Mama's arm. "I'll send them a telegram, Fanichka," he said calmly. "And I'll tell them you're coming right away."

"Yes, Faina," said Grandma. "You must go and be with your parents. They need you desperately. You have to make Nina's funeral arrangements—a very sad task. Oh, Lord! The priests will not allow her to be buried with Orthodox Christian rites. I'll pray for her poor soul!"

"Yes," Mama said, nodding and looking at me, smoothing my hair absently. "I have to be with them."

Mama left the next morning to be with her parents; her presence would surely be a consolation to them in this very difficult time. How courageous she was to travel alone on this arduous voyage. She spent several days in solitude on the train, silently watching the cold landscapes fly by outside and anticipating the difficult task that awaited her at the end of the journey. Comforting her parents over the death of her sister, she was sure, would be one of the most difficult things she would ever have to do.

She stayed with her parents for several weeks, helping them deal with the tragedy and settling any outstanding matters that Nina had left behind. She tried with all her effort to convince her aged parents to come to Japan, but they resisted; they wished to remain in China. They wished to stay in their own home where they were comfortable. The idea of relocating again was more than they could handle at that time.

After saying goodbye to them with a heavy heart, Mama embarked on her long trip home. She got on the train with a bag holding a few mementos of her sister—two small cross-stitch embroidered pillows and a silver teaspoon bearing Nina's initials, which I still have and treasure dearly today.

After Mama returned home, my parents made plans to move away from Kagoshima. The atmosphere in the city had become truly oppressive toward anyone who was not Japanese, and Papa's business was steadily declining as a result. Considering the recent events in our lives, it was no surprise that my parents were just tired of fighting it. Papa was able to quickly sell his business for a good price, and before long, we packed up all our belongings and left Kagoshima for good.

Our Life With the Russian Colony

In the late spring, my family moved to Kobe. Sasha had warned Papa that establishing a business there could be difficult, but my parents felt that it was at least a familiar place—they had lived there when they first came to Japan from Harbin—and decided to take a chance.

Kobe was a cosmopolitan city with a downtown area offering a variety of enterprises, including a very large department store called Daimaru, elegant hotels, many restaurants, and several European schools. Buses and streetcars dashed along the wide streets, where Mama was happy to finally be able to shop in her favorite stores as often as she pleased; when we lived in Kagoshima, she had only been able to visit them a couple of times a year. Besides, Kobe had a fairly large contingent of White Russians. There was a Russian church, a school and a social club that provided pleasant interchange and activities for the Russian families.

My parents rented a house on a hill in a lovely neighborhood, on Kitano-cho–2nd chome 8/6; the residents were mostly European and American, though there were some Russians as well. Ours was a charming and spacious two-story building with pale gray stucco walls. It featured pretty, dark green shutters, and large windows overlooking the city and the harbor. The house was almost overgrown with beautiful English ivy, which made it appear very European, perhaps even French provincial in style. Bordering the front of the house was a Japanese garden, an area filled with white stones and pebbles, creeping evergreens, pine trees, and the prized dwarf red Japanese maple. Mama was delighted to be living in a Western-style house at last, which had hard wooden floors to walk on instead of *tatami* mats.

Mama also found great pleasure in growing flowers in our new backyard. In Kagoshima, she had no opportunity for gardening, as we had lived in an apartment. Here, she was especially proud of her roses, which she tended lovingly. In the summer, we often had lunch in the gazebo, which was covered with multicolored morning glories. In the evenings, I loved to sit on the balcony of my parents' bedroom, listening to the sounds of the city and looking at the lights of the ships in the harbor.

Our home was four blocks from a public bath, which Mama and I enjoyed visiting from time to time. Even though the Japanese had baths in their houses, some went to the public baths once a week as an inexpensive social event. The public baths were not only for bathing and soaking, but also for conversing and gossiping, and maybe enjoying a good massage. Women usually went before dinner, men and boys after. The public baths' huge tubs were two-and-a-half-feet deep, surrounded by stone slabs where people sat to steam themselves. Mama and I would come out of the hot baths tingling all over, towel ourselves off, and leave for home all wrapped up to keep warm.

Papa started an exporting business, primarily stockings and other silk items; he even had some American companies as clients. As Sasha had said, the economic atmosphere in Kobe was difficult, and though later on he did quite well, Papa did struggle to build his business initially.

Hello Golden Gate — Goodbye Russia

I attended St. Mary's Catholic Church, where I took classes in the mornings in English. They offered French lessons in the afternoon, but I could not attend those, as they interfered with my Russian schooling. Several Russians had volunteered to form a part-time school and taught classes a couple of times each week, in the afternoons and on Saturdays.

In Kobe, the Russian school Christmas stage presentation. Klava is second from the right and I am the third, with dark stockings.

Each day, I walked ten blocks to St. Mary's and ten blocks home again. During this trip, I passed a German school where the students shouted "Heil Hitler!" and sang loud songs as they left on their bicycles. Any passersby who were not German or Japanese were pelted with stones, pushed, and threatened. I didn't like passing by this school, but I could not avoid that route, to my regret.

From the time we moved to Kobe, I made many new friends, including some who were Russian. My best and longest-lasting relationship was with Klava Volhontseff, a very sweet girl whom I still count among my friends today. We went to the same Russian school and attended some of the same social gatherings. My memory tells me that she lived far away, which made it difficult for us to play together often; we were too young to travel the distance unescorted. Klava lived with her parents and two younger brothers in what seemed like a tight Russian social circle. She now lives in California and we keep in touch by mail or telephone, often reminiscing about old times.

I did not only associate with Russian children in Kobe, however. My best friend for a while was Razilia, a girl from India. We lived across the street from each other and played at each other's houses, always conversing in Japanese, our common language. Because of our friendship, our families also tried to interact socially; my parents invited hers over for dinner, and in return, they invited us to eat at their house one night. We were new to Indian cuisine, but Papa loved everything they offered. Mama, on the other hand, couldn't swallow the spicy food and spat it out quietly into her napkin.

"Shura," she whispered, trying to hide her look of distaste. "How can you eat this? It's burning my mouth!"

Papa laughed quietly and patted Mama's arm. "Drink some water, Fanichka," he told her. "And stay away from the hot cucumber!"

Mama was gracious, of course, and did not say a word to our hosts about her discomfort. However, later on, when we returned home, she declared that she could never go back there again.

Razilia's family returned to India in the summer of 1941, and for a while, their house was empty. Sometimes I wandered into it, and the lingering aroma of their cooking spices made me cry. I missed Razilia very much and fantasized about living in exotic India, wearing gorgeous saris, with diamonds in my nose.

Another playmate, Helen, was two years older than I was. As her family was quite poor, she had only a few toys and rather shabby clothes. Once, she stole a set of toy dishes from me. I was convinced that she was the culprit of the horrible theft, and I walked into her house unannounced with my mother. We caught Helen playing with my dishes! Our two mothers had a big row, and I was forbidden to play with Helen forever. Well, "forever" lasted about a week, and we continued our rocky friendship from then on.

Other children stayed away from Helen, though I can see now that *she* was not the problem—it was the rest of her family, who were, as my mother noted, "unsavory." The father was a known drunk, her older brother was a thief who eventually died in prison, and her older sisters were prostitutes. After World War II, the girls married sailors and moved to

Portugal and Brazil. The rumor was that Helen went to Russia and became a member of a powerful Communist party.

Meanwhile, Helen was the friend who told me some of the difficult "facts of life." One of the most painful examples of this occurred during a Russian Christmas party. It was at a club, for all the children in the area; it was a great event that we all looked forward to every year. The tree was in the center of the room, and we held hands as we ran around it, singing songs. Then, Santa would come out with gifts. This particular year, as I watched the red-suited man taking the beautifully wrapped presents out of his enormous bag, Helen said, "There is no Santa. That man dressed up like him is your papa!"

I stopped in my tracks and glared at her indignantly. "No, no!" I cried. "You're lying!"

"Oh, *yes*!" Helen went on, a mischievous little smile on her face. "I'm telling the truth. Look at his mouth—he has two gold teeth in the front that are exactly the same as your papa's!"

I put my hands over my eyes; if this was true, I did not want to know. But Helen kept telling me to look and pulling at my hands, and so finally, I mustered the courage to take a peek. And oh, to my horror, Helen was right! Santa's teeth were the same as Papa's. I rushed out of the room, weeping and heartbroken. What a terrible way to find out that there really was no Santa.

Throughout our friendship, Helen continued to inform me of any other "facts" she felt I needed to know. It was from her that I learned about the "birds and the bees," and our female "monthly troubles." Eventually, I began to dislike Helen and tried not to associate with her anymore.

My third good friend in Kobe was Irene, whose grandfather had come to Japan in the 1920s and established a chocolate factory. When I met Irene, her grandfather was still running the factory as well as a candy store, with the help of Irene's father. During World War II, U.S. warplanes bombed the family's factory. Later, when America compensated Westerners in Japan for damages caused by the war, Irene's family was given an undamaged chocolate factory; it had once been owned by Germans and was confiscated by U.S. officials after the war. With this upgrade, they were able to sell chocolate all over Asia and became very wealthy as a result. That, at least, was the story told to Mama by some of her friends.

Chapter 6:
Being Stateless

The Two Sisters

Though we lived a fairly happy life in Kobe, one truth remained through it all: we were stateless. We had no roots, and no matter what country, city, or community we moved to, we would never be able to plant ourselves and fully grow. Our existence was essentially unpredictable; my parents were always aware that at any time, something could happen and we would have to pack up and run again.

The people of Japan were generally good to White Russians; they neither persecuted nor directly harassed us simply because of our ethnic background. However, life turned sour for everyone when Hitler invaded Poland. Refugees started coming to Asia from Europe, and though it seems like a strange situation, the Japanese allowed Polish and German Jews to enter the country if they had a sponsor and a place to stay. Our Jewish community, and some others, banded together to help these refugees; a popular saying at that time was, "If you have the room, you can save two lives."

One day in early March of 1940, my father's friend, Misha Shapiro, came to visit us. I liked him because he was a cheerful person, full of jokes and always bringing me candy from the delicatessen he owned.

"Olga!" he would usually boom as I waited to see what sort of confection he would pull from his coat pocket. "Sweets for a sweet girl!" he would say, laughing heartily and holding out a handful of treats, telling me to take them all if I wanted.

This time, though, he came empty-handed and looking very glum. He said hello to me quickly, then whispered briefly to my parents, who sent me out of the dining room. They all sat around the table, drinking tea from the *samovar*, while I went to the porch and listened to what they were saying.

"Death," Misha said. "Tragedy… refugees…" He told my parents many words that I did not understand, but I could hear him becoming very agitated. Mama started to cry, and after Misha left, my parents talked quietly together for a long time. Mama kept crying.

A few days later, my parents announced that two people would be coming to stay in our home. This meant that the three of us would have to move out of our two large bedrooms; my parents would take a smaller "guest room" and I would move next to them, into a large closet with one window. What was more, we would have to use the Japanese-style bathroom downstairs, as the large one on the second floor would be given to the new arrivals. Needless to say, I was very upset, and I was prepared to be quite unpleasant to these tenants, whomever they were, and whenever they arrived.

One lovely, sunny day in May, I came home from school and found Mama and Grandma having tea in the dining room with two ladies whom I did not recognize. Mama introduced them as Manya and Bronya Bauman, our new residents who would be staying upstairs. Bronya rose from the table and came to shake hands with me. She spoke Russian, but with a Polish accent; she had a sour look on her face, though her overall demeanor was quite proper. Her sister, Manya, remained seated at the table. She smiled and softly told me that she was very happy to be staying with us. Her eyes sparkled with a bit of tears.

At my mother's insistence, I sat down next to Manya, and it was then that I noticed the big hump on her back. I had never seen anything like it in my life except in *The Hunchback of Notre Dame*, but the man in that movie was awfully ugly. Manya was rather pretty, I thought, despite her physical deformity.

"Olga," she said to me, noticing that I was looking at her back, but smiling kindly at me anyway. "That's a lovely name. How old are you, dear?"

"I'm seven," I answered meekly, a little embarrassed that she had caught me staring.

"Seven!" Manya answered. "Why, I would have guessed you were at *least* nine. You look so grown-up for your age!" She smiled at me, and I had to admit that she was not at all like I had imagined she would be when I first laid eyes on her.

A little while later, Manya said that she was tired and needed to go to her room to rest. Mama, Chizuko, and Bronya took both women's suitcases and other belongings upstairs, and I followed behind. Poor Manya! Not only did she have a hunchback, but she was limping, and the 17 steps seemed very difficult for her to climb. By the time she reached the top, she was breathing with difficulty, the air going in and out of her lungs in great, noisy wheezes. I felt terribly sorry for her, though I, too, was feeling the same way. Bronya guided her sister to a comfortable armchair, into which she simply collapsed.

I slowly, shyly made my way over to Manya. "Do you have asthma?" I asked her. She nodded, yes, unable for the moment to speak to me.

"I also have asthma," I told her, and at that moment, I realized that I could never be unfriendly or nasty to her. I knew how it felt when breathing became difficult, and I knew that from that moment on, we would share a special bond.

Over the next few days, Manya and Bronya settled in comfortably. Bronya got a job downtown as a bookkeeper, and Manya, because of her illness, mostly stayed home and puttered around their rooms. As time went on, I visited her often, and she told me many stories about their lives.

In Poland, where the sisters were from, Bronya had been a professor of mathematics at a university; Manya had studied music and been a voice and cello teacher. Their parents had been quite wealthy, but they had died when Manya was 22 years old. Bronya was a bit younger, but she chose to spend her life taking care of her sister, and she never married. Needless to say, they were very devoted to each other.

When Hitler's government began to persecute Jews, the two sisters had to escape from their home in Poland. They fled to Russia, taking with them only a few important items, some clothing, and Manya's precious old Italian cello. They planned to support themselves by selling off their jewelry; alas, the Russians themselves were very poor and unable to purchase such extraneous items. In order to earn a few measly *rubles*, Bronya worked in hospitals, scrubbing operating rooms and floors as she and her sister moved from town to town. They made their way across the vast expanse of Siberia, hoping to reach Vladivostok, a seaport on the Pacific Ocean.

One day, as they traveled through a large city in Siberia, a music professor offered to buy Manya's cello. Just the thought of parting with her precious instrument was heartbreaking, yet they needed the money desperately. They had no alternative but to sell it so that they could continue on the rest of their journey. Eventually, they reached Vladivostok, where a ship took them to Japan. It was a very long, very rough expedition for them both, but in the end, they were happy to reach freedom together. My parents understood the sisters' plight, as they too had fled their homeland and become reluctant refugees two decades earlier.

As time went on, I became very fond of Manya, and I am sure that the feeling was mutual. She talked to me a great deal about music and played many records for me; she said she wanted to open for me the "window" to understanding classical music. Were there a piano in our house, she would have taught me how to play it, and in fact, she encouraged me to pursue vocal training when I grew up. She thought I had potential for a good voice, and believed that singing was beneficial for asthma sufferers, as it required great control of the breathing.

Manya seldom went out of the house, but one day she ventured on a shopping trip with her sister. She returned home with a present for me—a record of Viennese operettas sung by Erna Zach, who was very famous. I was thrilled to listen to her voice and I played the record over and over again.

Days went into months, and the winter passed. Spring came early in 1941, and we began to get ready for Easter. My mother baked the wonderful traditional breads called *kulichis*, as well as many other delicacies. It was also time for the Jewish Passover celebration, and Manya was busy cooking her own holiday specialties as well.

One day, as she worked on preparing these traditional foods, Manya called me into the kitchen. "I want to show you what I'm making for our holiday dinner," she told me. "It's called gefilte fish. And tomorrow night, my sister and I would like you and your family to come and enjoy it with us at our Seder feast."

I was so excited as we all went upstairs the next night. Bronya and Manya had also invited Misha Shapiro, who officiated during the ceremonial feast, as well as his wife. My mother had loaned Manya a lovely white linen cloth for their table, and I was eager to try all the different new foods that Manya had laid out on top of it.

I discovered that I loved gefilte fish—well, except for the horseradish—and since that night, I often think of Manya whenever I have the chance to partake of it again.

The two sisters lived with us a few more months. In the autumn of 1941, they left for Australia, where they hoped to find peace and a place they could settle down for good, at last. I was happy for them, and I said farewell with a smile, but when they were gone I was terribly sad, and I cried for many weeks. I missed Manya and the delightful hours we spent together, chatting and listening to records. The memories of those afternoons have stayed with me throughout these many years, and I will always be grateful to her for showing me how to open that "window" to the beautiful world of music.

Japan Attacks the U.S.

On the morning of December 10, 1941, Mama was clearing some broken twigs and sweeping dead leaves from the front of our house. She noticed several military limousines stopped at the end of our street, outside some houses occupied by English and Dutch families. As she watched, the men who lived in those houses were escorted out by Japanese officers, put into the limousines, and quickly whisked away. Mama paused and stared, puzzled by the speedy departure of the automobiles. She did not know what was happening, yet she had an ill feeling about the event she had just observed.

Though we did not know it until much later, that day—which because of the time difference was actually still December 7, 1941, in the United States—was when Japan attacked Pearl Harbor, and Mama was witnessing a direct result of that. The Japanese government did not release any specific information about the event, only the very vague statement that Japanese forces had overtaken Americans in Hawaii; we only found out what really happened, and how many had died, after the war was over and we were no longer in Japan. At this point, we only knew that Japan and the U.S. had entered World War II, nothing more.

Immediately following Pearl Harbor, the Japanese government was quick to remove any person they thought might be of some subsequent threat. This included American and Dutch businessmen, as many of our neighbors were. They were persecuted because they came from countries on the Allied side of the war. These men were taken from their homes and interned in concentration camps; the women and children were taken later. After that, there were restrictions for everybody.

The next month, on January 1, 1942, the Japanese celebrated their New Year; they always have it on that date, unlike other Asian countries whose New Years fall on different dates in January and February. It is the most important holiday in the country. People decorate their houses inside and out with bamboo, pine branches, and oranges, and celebrate with *o-mochi*, sticky rice buns roasted on charcoal and eaten with various sauces. Oh, how I loved the smell and taste of those delicacies!

Traditionally, on Japanese New Year, men from each family go from house to house, leaving their calling cards as a way of paying respect. The children spill out onto the streets; girls parade their kimonos and play *hagoita*, a badminton-like game with pretty, decorated paddles, and the boys all compete in kite-flying competitions.

That year, though, the mood was different—it was charged with patriotism, but the atmosphere was subdued. The military was everywhere. However, for us White Russians, life seemed basically unchanged.

Getting Out of Japan

With the start of World War II, Papa's import/export business with the United States ran dry. Given no other choice, we packed up and ran again; in fact, we left Japan only three days before the U.S. Air Force's first bombing of Tokyo. That event, like the entire war itself, was kept very secret and was not discussed on radio programs or in the newspapers. I learned about it much later, after the war.

Soon after the New Year, we began making plans to move to Shanghai, and eventually, we had to break this news to Chizuko. With a heavy heart, Mama called her into the living room one afternoon, and they sat down together. Mama was fighting tears, having trouble finding the right words to say.

"Chizuko," Mama began. "You know that our situation is very different now than it used to be. My husband will not be able to make a living in Japan anymore, so we'll be moving to Shanghai in April. We don't know what will happen in the future, or what awaits us in China. For that reason, we cannot take you with us, as much as we would like to."

Chizuko looked stunned, unable to utter any words.

Mama continued. "I spoke to my friend, Luba, since you like her very much. She would be delighted to have you live with her and her husband to help them with household chores, especially cooking. Will you take the job?"

"No, no!" Chizuko cried out. "I want to stay with you. I'll go anywhere with you! You don't have to pay me anything. I'll be happy as long as I'm with your family."

Unfortunately for all of us, Mama had to be firm about the decision. For several days, she cajoled Chizuko, who finally consented to work for Luba and her husband, Volodya. The couple was very close to our family, and even Chizuko had known them since our time in Kagoshima. Luba was, in fact, my godmother.

As the day of our departure drew near, painful and tearful goodbyes became a daily routine. Father was trying to keep a positive outlook, though he, too, broke down in tears a few times. Mama was completely distraught, walking around and packing up the house in an almost catatonic state, looking around at the growing piles of boxes as if through hazy eyes. Grandma was terrified to travel in her nonambulatory condition, and to live again in an unknown place. All the while, though, we tried to lighten the situation by reliving many fond memories of good and happy times, and sometimes, this seemed to help.

I was sad to leave our house and our gray cat, but most of all, I was heartbroken about moving away from Chizuko. The poor gal ran about the house packing our belongings with an insane frenzy. Her face resembled a creature from a Japanese ghost story, with an ashen pallor, glassy, sunken eyes, and her hair in disarray.

When the day of our departure finally came, we walked around the house one last time, touching a favorite corner or a beloved window and saying our silent farewells. We then got into a couple of taxis and departed for the train station. The train would take us to the port of Shimonoseki, where we would board a ship bound for Shanghai, China.

Chizuko came with us to the station; as was her character, she was still busy helping us even in those last, sad moments. She embraced us each one by one, valiantly fighting her tears until we climbed aboard the train. It was then that they began to pour uncontrollably down her face, as she ran alongside the departing train, waving to us with both arms.

Aboard the train, my father, brother, and I stood by the window, waving to her with all our energy. Mama turned her face away, unable to look. As the train moved faster, I pressed my wet face to the window, watching Chizuko's figure getting smaller and smaller until it was but a dot in the distance.

I cried as though my heart was breaking, and in truth, it was. I was crying goodbye to a wonderful and happy childhood in Japan, the country I called my own homeland.

Chapter 7:
Shanghai

We Arrive in Shanghai

View of The Bund, Shanghai.

Our ship finally docked in Shanghai, in a port that offered a stunning panorama of the Bund, a bustling area lying directly on the Wangpoo River. Our first view of the city, its tall buildings and busy streets were certainly impressive.

    Papa immediately rented a suite of rooms for us at the Metropole, a European hotel one block off the Bund; we were to stay there until he found us an apartment. After settling in, we went for immunizations against cholera, an annual summer scourge that affected the entire population of the area. We received identification cards to show that we had the shots, and my parents seemed a bit relieved after we were done with that unpleasant task.

    Mama spent a great deal of time on the telephone during those first days, trying to locate her old friends from

Harbin who now lived in Shanghai. To her great delight, she was able to get in contact with many of them.

One of the first friends Mama reunited with was Valia. Several years before, when Valia was 19, she had a job as a hostess at a fashionable restaurant in Shanghai. One of the regular patrons, a very rich and attractive businessman, was pursuing her; he showered her with gifts and asked her out on dates. Before long, she fell in love with him. As their relationship progressed, he set her up in an elegant apartment and took care of her every need, though he kept his own apartment as well.

A few years into their relationship, Valia became pregnant, and to her great joy, she gave birth to a beautiful baby girl. They named her Margarita and gave her Valia's last name because this wonderful, handsome man, whom Valia loved so dearly, had a wife and family in Holland, and he felt that giving the child his name would not be the right thing to do.

Not long after that, his wife decided that she wanted to visit Shanghai, to see the city that her husband had moved to for his job. The man quickly organized a trip to Kobe for Valia and little Margie, since he knew people there who would take care of them. He arranged for them to meet Luba, who worked at his friend's pharmacy in Kobe. Luba was my godmother, and that was how Mama and I made friends with Valia and Margie.

Valia was in her mid-20s when we found her again in Shanghai. A few days after our arrival, she and Margie came to visit us at the Metropole. She brought us a big box of chocolates from Dee Dee's, a very popular café and bakery. We greeted them both with open arms.

"How big you are, Margie!" Mama exclaimed, sweeping the girl up in a heartfelt embrace. "What a beautiful girl you've become, with all those gorgeous blonde curls. And you've inherited your mother's adorable dimples!"

"Welcome to Shanghai," Valia told us warmly, rushing to Grandma and hugging her. "We have to go quickly—there's so much I want to show Faina and Olga today. But I promise I'll be back to play some card games with you, Paraskeva, like we did in Kobe!" Grandma was completely housebound by then and unfortunately would not be able to join us on our afternoon outing.

Valia and Margie.

So off the four of us went. We climbed into a two-seater pedicab; our mothers bounced Margie and me on their laps for the course of the ride. We went through the International Settlement and then entered the French Concession, which was still run by the French government despite the Japanese occupation of its surrounding areas. It was made up mostly of houses and apartment buildings, though there were many small businesses, stores of all kinds, theaters, and restaurants as well.

We had lunch at Valia's beautiful apartment; her Russian cook prepared us an excellent meal. After we ate, Margie and I set about playing on the floor while Mama and Valia enjoyed some tea and conversation.

From the living room, I heard Valia sigh. "I miss him so much," she told Mama, her voice laden with sadness.

"Do you know where he is?" Mama asked.

"No," Valia replied. "He was taken to a concentration camp by the Japanese because he's Dutch—so many men from Holland have been taken away, as well as American and English men, too. He's in central China somewhere, that's all I know." I thought I heard her fighting back tears.

"Oh, Valia," Mama said sympathetically. "How do you manage here without him?"

"It's hard, Faina, and I can't do it anymore." Valia paused for a moment, and then went on to confess, "I have to give up this apartment. Margie and I will be moving into a small two-bedroom place with my sister, Mara. She's in a similar situation as I am right now. I suppose it will be good for both of us."

Later in the afternoon, we went for a walk along the elegant, tree-lined boulevard. Valia suggested we stop at Dee Dee's for coffee; Margie and I had hot chocolate and we all ate some of the most delicious French pastries we had ever tasted. When we had finished partaking in these delights, Valia engaged a taxi to take Mama and me back to the hotel. As the car pulled up to the curb, Valia told Mama quickly, "Don't trust the Chinese, Faina—especially any maids you hire. Thieves are everywhere. And make sure you set a price before you board a taxi or a pedicab or you'll end up paying twice as much as you should!"

Mama looked shocked as she watched Valia negotiate with the driver. In Japan, we seldom locked our doors; the notion that anyone and everyone could be looking to swindle us in Shanghai was almost unthinkable. After Valia set a price, Mama and I boarded the taxi and made our way back through the city. All in all, it had been an educational and delightful day.

The city of Shanghai was divided into three sectors. The Bund, where we were staying, was part of the International Settlement; all the big businesses were there, as well as hotels, the best restaurants, a large racecourse, hospitals, and a variety of residences. The streets were wild with traffic: rickshaws, bicycles, streetcars, pedicabs, and people raced around each other on what seemed to be an inevitable collision course. In the past, the British government had controlled the International Settlement, but after the beginning of World War II, it had been taken over by the Japanese.

Most Chinese people in Shanghai lived in the Hongkew, the Asian sector. Though we were unfamiliar with this area in our early days in the city, we eventually came to realize that most of it was filthy and decrepit. There was a large Japanese district within the Hongkew that was decent, but the rest of it was a slum.

The third area was the French Concession, where Valia and Margie lived. It was primarily residential, with wide, clean avenues and many art deco buildings. It was where much of Shanghai's Russian community lived; at that time, 50,000 White Russians lived throughout the city, and the kinship was very tight. They still observed all the important cultural traditions, and Russian social life in Shanghai truly thrived.

Russian Orthodox Cathedral in Shanghai

The pride and joy of Shanghai's Russian community at the time was a magnificent Russian Orthodox Cathedral, which was led by the great spiritual leader Archbishop John. The cathedral was a tall structure, about 10 stories high with 5 cupolas; it occupied almost a full square block. Adjacent to it was an orphanage that at any given time was home to over a hundred orphans, both Chinese and Russian.

Russians ran many of the city's small businesses as well as the symphony, the ballet company, and many nightclubs and restaurants. Some Russian Jews, who had filtered down from Harbin in search of better opportunities in the continental atmosphere of Shanghai, had owned many businesses.

After a few weeks at the Metropole, my father brought news that he had seen an apartment in the French Concession, in a beautiful high-rise building surrounded by a large, parklike setting. However, after asking the advice of friends who had lived in Shanghai for some time, he learned that the Japanese were planning to take over that building and convert it into a military hospital. After they occupied Shanghai, it seemed, Japan had commandeered many large apartment buildings and evicted any tenants who were not Japanese, sometimes even seizing their possessions as well.

Papa instead discovered a building across the street, on Avenue Haig, No. 209, where he purchased a large, four-room apartment on the second floor. We were all pleased to have found a new home within the French Concession; our building was located on a bustling, three-street intersection, but it had a quiet rear area with an abundance of tall, shady trees, and beyond that, another 10-unit apartment house where my friend Ronnie lived. There was no elevator in the four-story building, and since Grandma was not able to climb stairs, she was carried in a sedan chair up to our apartment. After that, she never left.

My family and I had loved living in Japan, where the atmosphere was generally peaceful and refined, the people always polite. We had immersed ourselves in the country's culture, becoming as much a part of it as we could without losing our own identities. In Japan, we felt like a part of the native people. In China, we discovered over time that we felt like foreigners. In Shanghai, we were truly the White Russian emigrants.

When we came to China, we heard about its great culture, but we were distracted from it almost immediately; the effort it took to just live our everyday lives in the new, chaotic environment kept us from ever really embracing its finer side. We did not have any Chinese friends because we were ultimately immersed in the Russian Community, and as always, the Russian culture. My parents had many friends within the community and sometimes had them over to our apartment to socialize. Some of the best gatherings they had included a man by the name of Alexandre Vertinsky, a Russian cabaret singer who wrote satiric songs that were very popular in Asia, Europe, and America. His records sold worldwide, wherever there were Russians. He lived in Shanghai both during and after the war, and then he went on to France; after that, he returned to Moscow to live there under the Soviet government. Rumor had it that he was famous enough to never be shipped off to Siberia.

In Shanghai, though, Papa did not have any business relations with Chinese, so we did not have opportunities to socialize with them that way, either. At one point, we did have Chinese neighbors who were politely pleasant, though we never became involved with them socially. We went to a museum to see Chinese artwork a few times, but never seemed to have the time to explore it further.

On the whole, Mama was the one put off most by life in China. She didn't even care for the food, though Papa loved it; overall, he was a little more easygoing about the whole experience of living in Shanghai. He sometimes took my brother and me to banquet restaurants, such as the popular Mayfair, where we met some of our friends. We would also on occasion have Chinese food delivered to our apartment by a small, nearby restaurant. For a fee, a deliveryman would bring the food in two baskets that hung from the ends of a bamboo rod across his shoulders.

We never ate inside the restaurant, but one day as I walked past it with Mama and our family's maid, we noticed that it was boarded up. A sign posted on the door read, "By order of the police." Mama asked our maid if she knew what had happened, and she told us that they had been selling dog meat, a practice that the Japanese frowned upon. Despite the somewhat gruesome details of the story, Mama obviously felt vindicated in her distaste for Chinese cuisine.

As time went on, we became at least a little more comfortable with our new life, once we learned the ins and outs of it. One of the first and most important things we learned was that the city's water was not potable. Bottled water did exist, but it was prohibitively expensive. Instead, we boiled whatever we needed to use every day.

Because we lived in a Western-style building, we were lucky enough to have indoor plumbing, while most Chinese homes in the city did not enjoy this luxury. Most Chinese families had no toilets; they instead used what they called "honey pots" to collect their bodily wastes. Early each morning, women would come out of their houses and empty these pots into the carts of vendors who would take the "human gold," as they called it, to sell to farmers as fertilizer. It was no wonder, really, that diseases ran so rampant across all of China. After emptying their pots, the women would rinse them out in the gutters, which explained the ever-present stench in many areas of the city. On many streets, men urinated on walls while children just squatted down on the street with the pants opened up.

Despite this decidedly unsanitary situation, there was an entire population of people who called the streets of Shanghai their home. They lived out their entire lives, from birth to death, in lean-tos and bamboo shacks. I walked by these makeshift constructions sometimes with my mother and was shocked when I realized that children lived in them, too.

I also remember seeing rickshaw men on meal breaks in the streets, picking lice out of their hair as they ate. Almost all Chinese seemed to be afflicted with the bugs and eager to get rid of them in public. Women would even sit outside on chairs, delousing each other's tresses with combs made especially for the task.

Even worse than lice, perhaps, were the bedbugs. They were a problem throughout the city, and for that matter, throughout China; from the poorest to the richest households, the pests seemed to spread wherever humanity lived. Once bedbugs got into the woodwork, it was almost impossible to get rid of them. They tended to die out in the winter, but the infestations in the summers were awful; alas, we could not escape them. Every summer my mother battled these pests using kerosene infused with hot peppers, which she smeared around the beds and floorboards.

My Illness: Asthma

As the summer came to a close and we fully settled in our new environs, it was time for my parents to enroll my brother and me in school. My brother went to St. Xavier's, a Catholic, English-language school; he was fluent in English already, as he had learned the language while attending the Canadian Academy in Kobe.

My mother decided to send me to a Russian school, one of the three in the city. I attended the small, all-girls school, which was highly regarded. A stern, aristocratic spinster ran the school, which she proudly modeled after the old Russian method.

The school's required dress was a purple wool pinafore with a black blouse, or a white one on special holidays. I enjoyed being among so many Russian girls and forming new friendships. I was proud to know some English, as most of the girls had a rather limited knowledge of that language.

The school year began well. My grades were excellent; the studies came easily to me. Good self-esteem filled my heart, and I was enjoying my life. Soon enough, though, things took a turn for the worse. The weather became increasingly harsh: November brought cold winds and rain day in and day out, and a permeating dampness covered the city. I began to have chest colds and asthma attacks, and had to skip school a day or two each week. Keeping up with the required work became extremely difficult.

My parents panicked. "What should we do?" they asked each other, racking their brains for a solution. It was apparent to us all that I needed a professional tutor, so Mama and Papa contracted a lovely, gentle woman named Tina to provide my at-home education. I went to the school to take exams every few weeks and managed to get good grades. In the late spring, when the weather again turned and my health improved, I went back to the school for regular classes. I was delighted to do so. Believe it or not, I did miss the place!

One of my great joys during that year came in the form of a big, black, shiny piano that my parents bought for my ninth birthday. One of my grandmother's old friends from Harbin gave me lessons at her house that I enjoyed immensely; less enjoyable was the nauseating stench that her 30 or so pet cats created. Since there was no animal neutering in China, they multiplied like crazy, and her house was truly overrun. She did clean up after them, but it seemed as though they were a hard lot to keep up with just because of their number.

In spite of that, though, I persevered; I was very proud of my lacquered, black piano and even enjoyed practicing for my lessons. At home, I performed for anyone who would listen—as well as for those who would not. I still have the books that I used while learning to play.

The summer of 1943 was a happy and playful season for me. I formed a good friendship with my neighbor Ronnie, a smart, mischievous boy with curly hair. His

mother was Russian and worked in a restaurant; his father, who had died of tuberculosis, had been French. Ronnie and I were friendly with two other Russian boys named Vova and Kolya. Together we made up the "four musketeers"; we climbed trees, played ball, skipped rope, and played cards and Shanghai Monopoly.

Our favorite game, though, was catching cicadas. The insects were abundant in the summer, easily found in the trees. To catch them we would put some sticky gum on the end of a long bamboo rod; all we had to do was touch it to the cicadas' backs and they would be stuck. We filled shoeboxes with the male insects, as they were the ones who sang. At the end of the day, we would compare who had the most, declare a winner, and let the cicadas go free.

Crickets were also a great source of interest, not only for us but for many people in China. They were sold in open-air markets in warm weather. Farmers came with boxes full of the big, green insects, and children would be allowed to purchase one as their pet for the summer. Mama bought one for me, along with a cute little cage to keep it in.

My grandmother and I talked to my pet cricket and fed it cucumbers, tomatoes, and lettuce. We enjoyed listening to it sing all day. Later in the summer, I began to notice that his chirping sounded weaker, and one morning, I found him dead at the bottom of his cage. This was normal—the same thing happened every year—and though I was distraught the first time I saw his lifeless little body, I soon learned to just say farewell to my transient pet and put the cage away for next year.

I did not have any girl neighbors, but it didn't faze me; I enjoyed the boys as playmates. My only girl friend was Klava, who had arrived from Kobe a few months earlier, to my delight. She lived in a small, terraced apartment with her parents and two brothers. Together Klava and I listened to

American songs and memorized all the words; we also read Russian novels together and talked about what it would be like to grow up someplace else. I always spoke of America, but Klava dreamt of Russia. We imagined where we would live when the war was over, and guessed that America seemed closest, and thus the most logical.

Klava and I saw each other fairly frequently, though we needed to take a streetcar to do so. That was an enchanting summer. I was certainly a free spirit!

At the end of the summer, I saw one of the strangest things, something that I can still picture very vividly in my mind. It involved my family's Chinese maid, a young woman who came to our home three times a week to help my mother with cleaning and laundry. I noticed from the first time I met her that she had small feet; when I asked Mama about it, she told me that the Chinese had a tradition of wrapping a young girl's feet in cotton to inhibit their growth. Though the practice was outlawed in the 1920s, many people still did it; wealthy women especially prided themselves on the tiny proportions into which they could mold their feet.

One afternoon, I went into the kitchen to get something to drink, and I noticed that the door to our small back porch was open. It was a hot day, so I approached the door to see if someone was there cooling off. Well, someone was—it was our maid, sitting on the porch, cooling her feet in a basin of water. She had taken the cotton bindings off her feet and when I saw the feet in the water, I was struck silent. I must have stared with my mouth open; they looked just like pigs' feet to me! I felt revulsion at the sight of this woman's crippled feet. I don't think I even gave her time to say a word to me as I turned around and ran right out of the kitchen.

In September, I returned to school with trepidation, hoping to stay the full year. I was happy to see my old friends—including Klava—and I made some new acquaintances as well. The cold weather came quickly that year, and to make things worse, the heat in our apartment was severely diminished. Japanese officials were confiscating any scrap metal they could find for their own military uses; therefore, they had taken the radiators and furnaces out of many Western-style buildings, including our apartment. On top of that, they were rationing coal, and we could only obtain enough to heat one room with a potbelly stove.

My mother decided that the stove should be in the living room, and she moved my bed there to keep me warm. My brother and grandmother slept in a glassed-in area next to the living room so they could share the heat. My parents remained in their bedroom, suffering through the cold nights together. We were all certainly thankful that we had brought our futon quilts from Japan—even our cat, Mika, was pleased when she crawled underneath one of them to keep warm.

Before long, I began having colds and asthma attacks again, and my parents were beside themselves with dismay. Mama took me to many different doctors and even to a Chinese hypnotist, on the suggestion of a good friend. I remember those sessions so clearly: His room was draped in red silk, gold Chinese letterings hung on the walls, and fierce-looking Chinese gods stared at me from all directions. He sat me on a huge, soft armchair, took out some shiny objects, lit incense candles, and began chanting and tingling bells. That terrified me, and the candles bothered my breathing; I was wide awake, shivering, and coughing. Indeed, his rituals kept me from being hypnotized! Mama insisted that I try to see him again, and I did, but without success.

Meanwhile, I was missing school more and more days every week. At that point, our good Russian doctor Ivanoff suggested I drop out of school, as it was truly detrimental to force the issue. I was crushed. I felt absolutely defeated and ashamed of myself; I wanted so much to succeed in school. As a child, I could not rationalize that what was happening was not my fault. I felt useless and ugly; I cried and cried. I loved the school, and the thought of never going back to it made me terribly, overwhelmingly sad.

Mama tried her best to console me, even teasing that I was lucky not to have to get up early as my friends had to. "You can sleep as long as you like," she would say to me. "And you don't have to go outside into the damp cold. Do you know that your friends have to wear gloves and coats in the classroom because the school has little heat, either? See, it isn't so bad to stay at home and have the teachers come to you as though you were a countess!" I tried my very best not to show my disappointment to her. She was so good to me.

Besides my Russian teacher Tina, my parents hired Mr. Gardenstein to teach me English and math. He was an Englishman of Jewish background who was married to a very beautiful Russian woman; although many similar men were taken to concentration camps during World War II, Mr. Gardenstein had escaped such a fate. The rumor was, Mama told me years later, that his wife was the mistress of a Japanese general. When the war began, the wife was able to convince this man to grant her husband more lenient terms. So instead of internment, Mr. Gardenstein was put under house arrest. For the duration of the war, he never left his home.

Mr. Gardenstein was an excellent teacher and a jovial man who always made fun of his own bald-headed, potbellied physique. I enjoyed his lessons and I was grateful for his suggestion that I see American movies to improve my English skills. A few prewar films were still being shown around town, and needless to say, that prescription put him on a hero's pedestal in my eyes.

Papa's Business

Though he had for a time enjoyed a successful working life in Japan, once we were in Shanghai, my father had to start all over again. He had reunited with many old friends from Harbin who now lived in Shanghai. He was contacted by a man named Ivashenko, who was a wheeler-dealer in various commodities. He approached Papa, saying he had contacts to obtain a large amount of scrap metal and asking if Papa could use his Japanese connections to get clients for the merchandise. My father had several letters of recommendation from Japan saying that he was an honorable and trustworthy man to do business with.

Papa worked as a liaison, negotiating the scrap metal sales between Japanese officials and Ivashenko, who represented the Chinese suppliers. He knew how to treat the Japanese—he respected their traditions and practices, and in return, they trusted him with their money. It took time to build these relationships, and it was a great honor for my father to have eventually gained their hard-won confidence.

Everything went well for a while; we lived comfortably on the money Papa earned. After several months of small but regular sales, Papa was able to acquire a contract with the Japanese for an enormous amount of scrap metal. Ivashenko demanded a large down payment, and Papa negotiated the transaction. He received the payment—in cash, as was usual—and all seemed to be going according to plan.

I must say that my father was in no way a naïve man; he did not blindly trust people, especially when it came to business matters. His partner in the scrap-metal business had been an old friend, which had been reason enough for Papa to think him reliable. In hindsight, it was also the factor that made what he did to my father most despicable and cowardly.

When Papa had secured the down payment, Ivashenko took it and ran. He disappeared with the cash and left Papa to explain to the Japanese officials—the ones whose difficult trust he had fought so hard to attain—that their money was gone and the deal was off. Needless to say, the officials were angry, and they were not very understanding of my father's situation. He was a partner in the business, they said, so he was responsible, too. Because they could not find Ivashenko, they had my father arrested and put in jail.

He was immediately taken to a local police station—which was at that time run by the Japanese military—and thrown in a small, barred cell. In those first hours, he paced the floor, trying to figure out where he had gone wrong. "How could I have been so stupid?" he asked himself. "How long I tried to win the honor of the Japanese, and here I had their admiration, their respect—their friendship! It's all lost now, all gone." He sat down finally, holding his head in his hands in utter despair. "Ivashenko, I trusted you," he cried. "How could you do this to me?"

Though he was fortunate, I suppose, to have been kept out of the large Chinese prison, Papa's time spent in the small jail was nevertheless extremely damaging to both his body and his mind. Because he had been trusted by the Japanese, when they thought that he had betrayed them, the penalty was severe. The punishment he received for his partner's crime was brutal: he was beaten, yelled at, demoralized, and broken.

Mama went alone to visit Papa every day at the jail, but on one occasion, she decided to take me along. I was frightened, but I missed Papa and wanted to see him very badly. When we arrived, he was in the general area of the police station, handcuffed to the chair on which he sat. Peering past him, I could see the cage in which they had been keeping him.

I rushed to his side and hugged him tightly, tears streaming down my face. "Papa," I said, "Oh, Papa." I did not know what more to tell him.

In any other situation, he would have swept me up in his arms and swung me around, singing "Olinka, Olinka!" to me in his beautiful voice. But here, instead of such a warm greeting, all I got was a weak "Hello, Olga." Papa looked flushed and distracted, and his hands shook; this certainly was not the confident, high-spirited man I had known my whole life.

Mama embraced him and kissed him. "Shura," she said gently. "I've brought you some food." She held out a jar of jam and some sweet bread that she had baked in the form of a large pretzel. Papa reached for them, but a Japanese soldier who had been standing nearby jumped up and practically knocked them out of Mama's hands.

"No!" the soldier shouted, grabbing the bread and throwing it onto the desk next to Papa's chair. He unsheathed a small saber that hung on his belt and began hacking the bread into small pieces. The knife terrified me, as did the soldier's shouting and his quick movements. I clung to Mama and tried to hold back fresh tears.

"Oh," said Papa, grasping the situation slowly, watching as the soldier decimated the bread. "They're looking for hidden weapons." We all watched as the Japanese soldier tore apart the bread my mother had made.

After a few moments, an officer came in from another room. He yelled at the soldier, "Stop it! Stop what you're doing!"

The soldier immediately stood at attention, visibly stiffening at the appearance of his superior. "Yes, sir!" he replied. The officer walked over to Papa and looked down at him.

"Please," Papa said very calmly. "Please, have a piece of bread. My wife made it."

The officer looked at Papa for another moment, and then he reached over and picked up one of the small pieces of bread that the soldier had chopped off with his knife. He put it in his mouth and said, "*Oishii desu*. (It tastes good.)" He then turned and silently walked out of the room.

Mama sat down on a chair in front of Papa; I remained standing at her side. "What are they feeding you here?" she asked him, as always concerned that he was not getting enough to eat.

"Rice gruel," Papa answered, a look of distaste on his face. "It's very coarse, very difficult to eat…and some hard chunks of pork."

Mama frowned and shook her head, looking intently at her husband's face. "Shura," she said after a moment's pause.

"You look feverish, and you have red spots on your face. Are you feeling poorly?"

"No, Fanichka, no," Papa assured her quickly. He lifted his hand as if to wave away her concerns, but then remembered with a jolt that it was handcuffed to the back of his chair. He sighed, looking at the metal restraint that dug into his wrist. "It's just too hot in here. I'm sweating all the time."

The officer entered again. "Time to leave," he told Mama.

Mama smiled at Papa and assured him that she would return the next day.

"No," said the officer. "Come next week. We have new rules now."

As we walked out of the station, Mama looked very worried. "It was not hot in that room," she said to me. "I think Papa is sick."

The thought was almost too much for me to bear. "Mama," I whispered. "What can we do?"

"I'll talk to Dr. Ivanoff tomorrow. Maybe he can visit Papa." Tears welled in her eyes as she added, "Oh Olga, I'm terribly worried! Oh God, something is wrong!"

First thing the next morning, Mama got in touch with Dr. Ivanoff. Fortunately, he was able to see Papa within a couple of days, but unfortunately, he confirmed Mama's worries: Papa was very ill, probably with typhoid. This explained his feverish complexion and his complaint that the food at the jail was too rough for him to eat—typhoid inflames the intestines, and anything harder than liquid would have literally ripped him up inside. Dr. Ivanoff advised Papa not to eat any more of the gruel offered to him at the jail, as it was very dangerous for him to do so.

By the next week, when Mama was allowed to visit Papa again, he had already been transferred to a prison hospital, where he stayed for another week. At that point, the Japanese officials who ran the hospital called Mama and told her she had to come bring Papa home; he was very ill with typhoid and peritonitis, and they had given him up for dead. To get him off their hands, they called Mama and simply said, "Take him home."

When Papa returned home, Dr. Ivanoff took good care of him, with Mama's assistance; two Russian nurses whom Dr. Ivanoff knew from World War I helped him recover as well. I especially remember the nurse named Vera, who had lost her leg during that terrible war; Mama became very close to her and they remained friends even after Papa was well. They fought Papa's fever and gave him nothing but chicken broth to eat. It was a very difficult time for us all; we thought he could die at any moment. The fact that he did not was a miracle, and a testament to the excellent care provided by Dr. Ivanoff.

During this time, Grandma suffered a terrible emotional strain. It was understandable—her only beloved son was nearly on his deathbed. When he came home from jail, I was standing in our apartment with my grandmother; she was shaking, and tears ran down her face. "My son," she sobbed, "my little boy!" I seldom saw her cry, and it unsettled me. She was normally a woman of steel.

Papa recovered physically, in time. But mentally, he was never the same. The emotional damage done to him in the jail stayed with him for the rest of his life. Where once he was full of life and laughter, with a kind, outgoing demeanor, after this ordeal he was a sad soul, depressed all the time, an empty shell of the man he used to be. Even Ivashenko's capture and imprisonment some time later—and Papa's subsequent exoneration—had no effect on his emotional state. The damage was already done, and nothing could change it. My father as I had known him for the first 10 years of my life essentially ceased to exist.

Chapter 8:
War in Shanghai

Seeing the War Firsthand

During World War II in Shanghai, many of life's necessities were in limited supply—not just the coal we used to heat our apartment, but various foods and household supplies as well. Whereas in Japan, before the war, we could simply walk down the street to a store and purchase things we needed, in Shanghai we were forced to stand in lines and trade coupons for basic, everyday products.

First, we had to wait in one line to get the coupons for the rations, then in another line for the actual products. When Mama grew weary of it, I would go and stand in various queues by myself. I was not afraid to do this, as the Chinese were usually nice to a child standing on the rations line. I once met a Chinese man in a rice line who surprisingly spoke a bit of Russian. "Do you need soap?" he asked me. "I don't need soap, don't wash."

"Sure," I told him, a little taken aback at the idea that this man did not bathe. He held out his soap coupons to me, but I did not have money for buying extras; instead, I offered him some of my rice coupons. He seemed pleased with the trade, but when I got home, Mama was understandably not quite as happy about it.

Vegetables and fruits were thankfully still abundant in open markets, but dairy products, meats, and rice were rationed. Milk was especially difficult to obtain, which presented a problem for me: Due to my asthma, Dr. Ivanoff wanted me to drink a half-pint of milk per day, but we sometimes did not have even that small amount. Instead, I had to drink soybean milk; it tasted awful, but it was sustaining and very nourishing. When we could get regular milk, it had to be boiled, as pasteurization did not exist at the time in Shanghai.

Since meat was hard to obtain as well, Mama came up with some inventive recipes with eggplant, potatoes, and mushrooms. There was generally enough bread to go around, and honestly, despite the rationing, anything could be bought for the right amount of money; Shanghai's black market really thrived during that time. Few people starved except for the impoverished Chinese because of lack of food—it was usually lack of work (and therefore lack of money) that caused such dire situations.

As if it were not enough for the Japanese government to limit the public's consumption of necessary heat and sustenance, they also cut off our access to hot water. Before the war our apartment had hot water, however, Chinese dwellings usually had only one cold-water tap. Some affluent Chinese families did install the extra plumbing to bring hot water into their homes, and some even lived in European-style buildings that already had these amenities; most, however, just went without it.

Generally, Chinese people did not regularly take baths anyway, especially the women. They washed themselves, but they did not have tubs for bathing and soaking. During the war, the Japanese tried building public baths in Shanghai, but the idea was not met with much success.

After the radiators and furnaces were removed from our apartment building, we had to purchase hot water for bathing from—believe it or not—hot-water shops. These shops were an integral part of Chinese existence and were found nearly on every block. As part of the purchase, a Chinese man would deliver the water to our house with a bamboo pole balanced across his shoulders, a large bucket dangling from either end. Usually, Mama would enlist several men to bring four or six buckets, which would fill our bathtub about a third of the way.

Because the hot water was in such limited supply, we had to share it. I washed first, and then Mama took her own bath in the same water. My father and brother went through the same routine on another day of the week. My grandmother, with her crippled legs, could not bend her knees enough to step over the side of the tub, so I helped bathe her in a shallow basin that she could step into more easily. It was a chore I greatly disliked.

Mama had a friend at that time named Raya Sherlaimoff, whose husband, George, was a fire chief in the city. They lived in a spacious, well-heated apartment above the firehouse that, to their great fortune, had hot running water. Our occasional visits with Raya were always pleasant; Raya was a very generous person, and she always had delicious cakes and chocolates for us when we visited her for tea.

One day, Mama and I took a rickshaw to Raya's apartment, which was not far from our own. While we drank tea and enjoyed the warmth of Raya's sitting room, Mama related how during the previous week, she and I had taken our baths on a frigid day and had both caught colds. Raya was shocked—she did not realize that people had difficulty taking baths! Because she lived in a warm place and had access to hot water whenever she pleased, she took it for granted that others had the same amenities.

In keeping with her generous nature, Raya did not hesitate to share her luxuries with Mama and me. She offered us the use of her bathtub whenever we needed it, and from that time on, until the warmer spring weather came around, we went to Raya's every week to take baths. I remember the pleasure I felt while soaking in the hot, steaming bathtub—something that I had missed the last couple of years. I was especially happy to partake in these ablutions because by that time, my hair had grown very long—my tresses fell below my waist, and I had to use a lot of hot water to wash them. After drying my hair, I would plait it into two braids, tying the ends with lovely silk ribbons.

Me, age 14, before my haircut

Raya was a lovely, sweet lady, and for her generosity and kindness during that cold time in our lives, we were certainly most grateful.

Early in 1943, the American forces began bombing factories and oil fields on the outskirts of Shanghai. It was our first taste of the reality of World War II, and of course, we found it terrifying; the sirens blared almost daily. My parents seemed to be in a constant state of worry; they kept emergency bags of clothes and supplies packed just in case the bombs hit too close to home and we were forced to evacuate.

Japanese control in Shanghai became quite restrictive around that time, as Mama and I witnessed one summer afternoon while we shopped in the International Settlement. As we strolled down the street, looking in shop windows and enjoying our time out together, Japanese military officials and health authorities suddenly swooped in and cordoned off the area. They went from person to person, demanding to see cholera-shot certifications and giving inoculations to those who could not produce them. Everyone in the city was required to carry these IDs at all times, but as we soon realized, we had mistakenly left ours at home that day.

When the Japanese officer came around to us and demanded our certificates, I begged him in Japanese to let me run home to get them. He seemed taken aback that I knew his language, and I was sure that if I had not, he would not have let me go. He made Mama wait exactly where she was until I returned—four hours later—but once I produced proof that we had received the shots, we were released. In all, it was a very good lesson learned; we never left home without those certificates again.

My friend Ronnie and I, though our parents' fearful demeanors did unsettle us, found the air raids that took place in Shanghai fascinating. We would often go up to the rooftop garden of our building with Ronnie's binoculars to watch the airplanes fly in the far distance. He was an expert on the different kinds of aircraft and could identify which were American and which were Japanese based on the insignias painted on their sides. We often cheered for the planes; we were decidedly on the side of the Americans. It was during this exciting and frightening time that I realized that I no longer wanted to be Japanese. Ronnie and I daydreamed about going to America someday.

Most of the time, Mama would rush up to the roof and drag Ronnie and me back downstairs. "It's too dangerous, children," she would anxiously yell at us. "Why do you insist on going up to the roof when I've already told you how much it worries me? You could be hit by the anti-aircraft shrapnel they're shooting from the tall buildings in the area." The troubled expression on her face would make me feel very bad; she seemed to have that look very often at the time.

Papa had the same expression, as the wartime situation did nothing to alleviate his ongoing depression. I suppose that at my age, I did not fully comprehend the seriousness of the war, and I know that my parents tried to shield me from it as much as they could. Sometimes, however, I would overhear their conversations, and the things they talked about frightened me.

"An American plane," I heard Mama tell Papa one evening as they sat in front of the potbelly stove, drinking tea and talking quietly. I was huddled under the quilt in my bed, supposedly sleeping. "It was headed toward the river, to drop bombs on the ships. One missed the target and fell near the Bund instead."

"Oh, God," Papa replied in a distressed tone of voice. "There must have been many people hurt—the Bund is always so busy." I could see him shake his head in the dimly lit room. "Fanichka," he said to my mother. "When is it going to end?"

Our Menagerie of Tenants

By the early winter of 1944, our life had become very difficult. We had no heat in our apartment; we lived in the one room with only the potbelly stove to warm us. Papa no longer had a business, and my parents were forced to sell some of our valuables to survive. Mama would decide what to sell, but she was too ashamed to go to the pawnshops. Instead, I often did it for her. I felt terrible about giving up our beautiful pieces of silver and crystal, but I realized that it had to be done.

As the bombings in Japan began to escalate and most of the foreigners were sent to villages and provinces, many Russians who still lived there began to move to Shanghai. My godparents, Luba and Volodya, decided to make their move earlier, in 1943. Their comforting presence was very welcomed during the difficult time, and aside from their companionship, they helped us in any practical ways they could. Aunt Luba was a kind friend to my mother, providing levity or a shoulder to cry on whenever Mama needed one. Uncle Volodya helped us by negotiating the sale of some of our more precious valuables to wealthy Russians in the area.

The first thing we sold was my beloved piano; it was wrapped up and heaved out of one of our apartment's large front windows as I watched, heartbroken, my dream of becoming a musician shattered. Another day, Volodya came and told my mother that he had a buyer for our silver *samovar*. The last teatime we had before the man came to pick up our old trusted friend was a very sad occasion indeed.

Since we had a limited supply of possessions to sell, my parents had to look for other ways to secure an income. They decided after a short while to rent out our apartment's two empty front rooms that faced the street. They were spacious and clean and would certainly be attractive to someone in need of a temporary place to stay.

Mama turned to a local Jewish organization for help in finding potential tenants. She knew that there were Jews in the city who might be looking for lodgings, and she was right in that respect. By that point in World War II, several thousand Jews had come to Shanghai to escape Nazi persecution and find refuge. Hitler's reach was very long, however, and through Japanese cooperation, the Germans were able to keep the newly arrived Jews under control. They were all required to live in a ghetto in the poor and filthy Hongkew district; the military patrolled the area and the Jews could only travel to other parts of the city during the day. At night, there was a strictly enforced curfew.

To escape this plight, some of the Jewish refugees tried to find "indispensable" jobs; if their employment was deemed essential, they might be granted permission to move out of the Hongkew and live in another part of the city. This was the case with our first boarder, a man by the name of Fred Fobar.

Fred was a bachelor, a German, and a violinist. He played with the Shanghai Symphony and at several nightclubs—Japanese officials found his employment to be worthwhile, so he was given permission to rent a room from us to live in the French Concession. He was a meticulously dressed man who often spent a long time grooming himself in the bathroom, as I remember. His demeanor was charming but quiet. My father was very happy to have a fellow classical music aficionado around, and they sometimes discussed their favorite recordings and performers in their limited English. Fred loved to practice his violin in his room, and it gave us a great deal of pleasure to listen to him. Fred lived with us for many years, even after the war ended.

Our other empty room was intermittently occupied by a variety of tenants. One time, we rented to a non-Jewish German man who had escaped to Shanghai—not because he feared persecution, but because he strongly disagreed with Hitler's tyrannical practices. The man lived with a beautiful Chinese woman who was an excellent cook and taught Mama how to prepare some Viennese dishes. After they had lived with us for a while, we learned that her companion had been stricken with tuberculosis; that terrified Mama because I had asthma and was susceptible to various illnesses. She felt badly about it, but Mama campaigned to get them out of the apartment, because my well-being, of course, came before any of our tenants. The couple did leave, and sadly, we heard that the man died shortly after.

Next, we rented to a vivacious Jewish couple. They had been entertainers in Poland and knew many Yiddish songs, which they taught to me with great enthusiasm. I especially remember a song called "Baranovich," which was about a *shtetel*, a small Jewish village in Poland. The couple spoke excellent Russian and always seemed happy and full of life. They came and went, though; they did not stay with us for long.

After that, a Japanese woman and her two-year-old son, Masahide Komatsu, came to live in our second bedroom. The woman's husband was in Java, in the military. Mama befriended her, and I adored her boy, nicknamed Masa-chan. I showered him with affection, cuddling, hugging, and kissing him. In those days, the Japanese did not express emotions as Westerners did—they were not physical with their children, even though they loved them enormously. His mother allowed me to babysit him often; I took him for walks and tried to teach him a few simple Russian words.

Masa-chan would always run to my bed first thing in the morning, while Mama was making breakfast for our family. She would also cook for this Japanese woman occasionally, as the woman was pregnant and felt too ill to manage it herself. One day, as Mama cooked breakfast in the kitchen, Masa-chan's mother came in to retrieve the boy from our room. For one reason or another, I innocently decided that it was the right time to share my knowledge of Japanese aircraft with her.

"Do you know the difference," I asked her, "between Japanese planes and American planes?"

The woman, who had been bending over to pick up Masa-chan, stopped for a moment and looked at me. "No," she said slowly. "What is the difference?"

Sitting on my bed, I straightened my posture, happy to have this opportunity to show her how much I knew about the subject. "Well," I began, "Japanese planes are made of wood—they are very old-fashioned. American planes are made of metal, so they're much more sturdy. That's why they usually win in an air fight."

The woman stood up straight suddenly, heaving Masa-chan up and onto her hip. "That is very interesting," she said quietly, not looking at me. "Please, excuse me." Then she silently turned around and walked out of my room.

When breakfast was ready that day, Mama wondered where Masa-chan and his mother were. She told me to go fetch them from their room, but when I knocked on the door, there was no answer. Mama shrugged when I reported this to her. "Maybe she decided to go back to bed," she said, nodding her head. "Carrying a baby can be very tiring, you know."

By that evening, Mrs. Komatsu had not emerged from her room, and of course, Mama was concerned. When she knocked on the door of the woman's room, she did hear a meager "We are fine, thank you," but she was not invited to enter. When they did not show up for breakfast the next morning either, Mama began to suspect that something was very wrong. She marched down the hallway to their door and rapped on it loudly.

"Hello?" she called through the door. "Please, come out and let me know that you're both alright!"

The woman opened the door very slowly, and the look on her face was not exactly welcoming. "We are fine," she said again. "Thank you for your concern."

Mama smiled warmly. "Good," she said, "good. I was so worried that you weren't feeling well! But tell me, please, why have you not left your room in more than a day?"

The woman looked at Mama but did not say anything for several moments. Then she looked toward where I stood, half-hidden behind Mama. "Your daughter," the woman said. "She told me all about the *superiority* of American airplanes over Japanese airplanes, about how easily the Americans can shoot our planes out of the sky." She looked back at Mama's face. "How can someone who claims to have loved Japan so much teach their child something like that?"

Mama looked down at me, eyebrows raised. "Olga," she said, "did you say these things?"

I looked down at my feet until Mama reached down and brought my chin up with her hand. I sighed. "I did, Mama. I said it." The other woman's face seemed to relax a little.

"And where did you hear this information?" Mama went on.

"From Ronnie!" I confessed. "He knows everything about airplanes and that's what he told me." I looked at Masa-chan's mother. "I'm sorry," I told her. "I didn't mean to offend you!"

The woman looked at me for a moment, and then turned toward my mother. "So you did not tell her these things?"

Mama smiled again, almost laughed. "No, no," she said gently, pulling me around in front of her. "Ronnie is Olga's friend, she admires him so much. I think she was just trying to impress you with her knowledge!"

The woman smiled then as well. Mama had certainly broken the ice, and I was thankful for it. I felt awful that this whole problem had been my fault, and I had not even meant for it to happen.

"Will you please come out and join us for breakfast?" Mama asked.

The woman nodded, and Masa-chan ran out of the room and directly into my arms. "We would be delighted," said his mother, "thank you."

Everything was pleasant with Masa-chan and his mother after that. She turned out to be a very generous woman, sharing with us her extra coupons for rice and milk when she could. Before she left us she delivered her baby, and it was another handsome boy. They stayed with us for about a year, until the war was over. When it was time for them to return to their devastated homeland, our farewells were warm but melancholy. We all felt sadness because we knew we would never see each other again, and because we knew it was the end of an era for Japan. Masa-chan cried when they left, and so did I; he was, after all, another on the long list of people I would miss.

The War's End Is Near

In the early months of 1945, we began hearing rumors that World War II was going to end soon. Though this was not publicized in the local Russian newspapers, many of us received information over shortwave radios, which picked up Russian and American broadcasts. They said that the Hitler regime was on its last legs; of course, this news made us all very happy. Ronnie's mother wept about it, hoping it meant that they could soon go to France, the home country of her late husband.

There were other rumors, however, that the end of the war would bring with it the destruction of Shanghai. We did not know what was true and what was not; there was a real sense of being on pins and needles, a very restless feeling. We would sometimes hear bombs in the far distance and wonder, *Is this it? Is this the devastation we've been waiting for?* My parents kept the satchel containing our most basic belongings near their bed in case we had to get up and run in the middle of the night.

My parents prepared me for such a situation, telling me what I should do if we suddenly had to leave our home. Though we were all scared of the idea, what worried us most was Grandma—she could barely walk, much less run, with her crippled legs. What would we do with her if we had to evacuate on a moment's notice?

"Don't worry," she told my parents calmly, as she had already considered the matter. "I'll sit quietly and wait for my end." Her response startled my parents, and unsettled them;

they were not sure if they could really just leave her there if ever an emergency arose.

Throughout this difficult time, Mama tried to make the best of things for our family. She and I had a pleasant outing that we sometimes indulged in, a respite from the real world that was very special to us both. We would take an afternoon off from whatever else was going on in our lives and go see a movie together—we loved American movies, especially the MGM musicals—and then head to a café for something sweet. Sometimes we went to Dee Dee's, the very popular café that Valia had taken us to when we first arrived in Shanghai. More often, however, we visited the Continental Café. Wherever we went, we always had the same thing.

"I would like a Viennese coffee," Mama would tell the waitress, "with a little extra cream, please. My daughter will have a hot chocolate, and we will share a cream puff." After the waitress went to prepare our drinks, Mama turned to me and smiled. She always looked happy during our afternoons out together—they were truly special times, moments of mother-daughter closeness, when we allowed ourselves to enjoy a bit of luxury.

"Olinka, did you like the movie we saw today?" she asked me.

"Oh, yes!" I answered. We had seen *The Wizard of Oz*, and I had watched every second of it mesmerized and enchanted. "It was wonderful. I loved it! Did you, Mama?"

Mama nodded. "I did," she said. "Judy Garland is so cute and sings beautifully, don't you think? And the Wicked Witch was so scary!" She raised her hands like claws and leaned toward me, making a witchlike face; I recoiled, giggling.

The waitress came back with our refreshments. We picked up our forks and immediately dug into the cream puff, slowly savoring the first bite.

"I liked when it was all in color, Mama," I said, referring to the scene in *The Wizard of Oz* where the movie changed from black and white to Technicolor—a truly innovative trick.

"I did, too," she agreed, stirring her coffee slowly. "Olga," she continued, "wouldn't it be nice to be able to just click your shoes together and go home? With all the people you love right there by your side?" Mama smiled at me again, though her expression looked more downhearted than it had before.

I thought about it for a moment, and I knew exactly what she was saying. The only place I had ever thought of as my home was Japan, but I thought my mother might be referring to her family's *homeland*, Russia. Either way, it was strange to think of our life in Shanghai as nothing but a dream from which we would someday wake up.

"That would be nice, Mama," I said, smiling sweetly at her; I did not want to see her looking sad again, not while we were having our special mother-daughter time. I picked up a forkful of cream puff and held it out to her. "Here," I said. "Have a bite. I think this might be the best cream puff we've had yet!" I told her enthusiastically.

She took the bite of cream puff and we continued to talk about the movie, as well as other movies we had seen together. This tradition of ours continued for a long time—after the war, and after we left Shanghai, and right up until the end of my mother's life. Although she did not go out much in her final years, occasionally I would bring her a cream puff. We would sit together, share the sweet treat, and reminisce about all the cream puffs we had eaten together, all the movies we had seen, and all the good times we shared in spite of any hardships that had befallen our family.

Of course, we knew that we were not the only ones who suffered because of the war. There were certainly families in far worse situations than we were. For example, there was Tina, my longtime tutor. She always came to our apartment for my lessons, so I had never seen where she lived. Mama knew her address, however, so one afternoon we stopped by to drop off some of my homework.

Tina lived in a brownstone that had been divided up into rooms, each rented out to a different person or family, with one shared bathroom per floor. I followed Mama up a flight of stairs and we found the door that was supposed to be my teacher's apartment. Mama knocked, and Tina opened it right away, though she then immediately stopped short, putting a hand up to her heart.

"Faina," she said, her voice sounding genuinely surprised, "Olga. What are you doing here?"

"I came to give you my homework!" I announced proudly, holding the papers out to her.

Tina reached out slowly and took the homework from me. "Oh, Olga, very good," she said. She was standing against the wall with the door just slightly ajar so that we could not see inside; she glanced back into her room for a moment, then turned back to us and smiled.

"Where are my manners," she said nervously, slowly swinging the door fully open. "Please, come in."

I was delighted to finally get to see where my teacher lived, but as soon as she opened the door wide, I stopped short: her room was actually the bathroom. The tub had been removed, and in its place was a cot where Tina and her five-year-old daughter slept. There was a table and a couple of chairs, but little other furniture. The floors and walls were still covered with white ceramic tile; it was a cold, uninviting place, a long and narrow room with little leeway to move around. I could not believe that this kind, gentle woman lived in such an uncomfortable, desolate place.

It must have been obvious to Tina how shocked I was, and looking back, I feel sorry for that; I liked her so much, I did not want to make her feel bad about this living arrangement. I went tentatively inside, where Tina offered Mama and me the seats at her table; she sat on the cot and introduced us to her little girl, who was just as sweet as could be. After spending a little time there with them, I became more comfortable, and it appeared that Tina did as well.

Tina was a schoolteacher who received a very low salary, and even with her tutoring income, she did not earn much. My family discreetly gave her food as well as clothing that I had outgrown, for her daughter; her hard work and a little charity helped her survive World War II in Shanghai.

Mama had many old friends from Harbin who were living in Shanghai at the time, and most of them endured many hardships as they struggled to survive. One particular person comes to my mind: Nadya, a woman who had fallen virtually to "the lower depths." She had been a countess in Russia, born to privilege and extreme wealth, only to lose everything as she and her family fled their country. Along the way, Nadya made some poor choices—she married badly and allowed herself to be abused and abandoned. By the time Mama saw her again in Shanghai, Nadya was an alcoholic and a drug addict, living as a pauper in dingy rooming houses.

Although we were always short of money at the time, Mama had a kind heart, so she helped Nadya by offering her miscellaneous chores around our house—ironing curtains, for example, or sweeping cobwebs from the ceiling corners. Because Mama knew that whatever money she gave her friend would go directly toward a bottle of liquor, she instead paid her with food.

One wintry morning after Nadya had been working for us for a while, I awoke to the sound of my cat, Mika, meowing. I felt her stirring around my feet under the futon cover, and then she slithered out and jumped off my bed.

"Okay," I whispered. "I know, you want to go to your sandbox in the kitchen." I opened my eyes, and I could see the sky colored with pink streaks—the dawn was just breaking. I looked across the room, to where my parents were still sleeping peacefully. They had moved into the living room in early January, because Mama wasn't able to get any extra coal to heat their bedroom anymore. Papa was still recovering from his illness and needed to be in a warm place. So now, we all were quartered in one room, crowded yet cozy, trying to make the best of our circumstances.

Meow, meow, persisted Mika.

"Okay, shh," I told her as I dove into my heavy, quilted robe and fur-lined slippers. We quietly snuck out of our room; Mika dashed toward the kitchen, and I walked across the hall to the unoccupied front room to see how much snow was on the ground from the previous night's storm. I looked out of the big French windows and found that it was not much, just a dusting. The street was still quiet, just a ʻ, and a couple of pedicabs moving about.

Well, I should go back to bed, I thought. But just as I was about to turn away from the window, something outside caught my eye. Was that…a *person* lying in the intersection, by the old flagpole? *Why would anyone want to lie down over there*, I thought, *and who is it?* The person's ratty old fur coat looked familiar, and when I looked closer, I recognized the hat—a red knit cap with a pom-pom.

"Nadya!" I gasped. It was my mother's friend! I remembered that Mama had given her the red hat.

I knew right away that I must wake my parents and tell them that Nadya was sleeping in the street. I rushed back to our room and shook them excitedly.

"Mama, Papa, wake up!" I told them. "Nadya is outside. She's lying in the street—she must be hurt or something. Help her!"

My parents jumped up and rushed to the window to see what I was talking about. As soon as they scrutinized the situation, they looked solemnly at each other. My father quickly dressed and ran outside, taking Mr. Wong, our apartment's superintendent, with him. Mama went back to our room to restart the embers of our potbelly stove. I went back to the windows in the front room and saw that Papa was standing over Nadya and crossing himself.

Mr. Wong came back inside, urgently banging on our door. As Mama let him in, he said, "Missy! Call police, I give you number!" Mama dialed the number he recited on the wall phone in the hallway, but then gave it over to Mr. Wong, telling him that he had better do the talking, as her Chinese was not so good. Mr. Wong grabbed the phone and proceeded to excitedly relay his message to the police.

Mama got dressed so that she could go outside with Mr. Wong when he was done with the phone call. Just before she walked out, she went to our apartment's Beautiful Corner and picked up a small icon, which she took outside with her. From the window I saw her walk out into the intersection and stand next to Papa and Nadya; they both bent down, and Mama placed the small icon inside Nadya's coat and made cross signs over her again. Mama began crying. When the police arrived, they put Nadya into the paddy wagon and swiftly departed.

When my parents came back inside, I bombarded them with questions: "Where did they take her? How is she? Did they take her to a hospital?" Mama quietly sat me down at the table and looked at me with tears in her eyes.

"Olinka," she said softly, "Nadya died in the street last night. She froze to death. She will never come to see us again."

I stared at Mama, trying to understand the meaning of what she had said to me. The realization that a human being could actually *freeze to death* was an awesome concept for me to understand.

Mama was very sad about her friend's demise; she always said that it was not a fitting end for an aristocrat, such as Nadya had once been.

Though we had heard that the war was coming to an end, we did not know when it would happen; we simply continued on with our normal lives as best we could and waited for more news to arrive. My family and I continued standing in lines for provisions and huddling around our potbelly stove to keep warm; Ronnie and I continued watching planes on the rooftop and entertaining ourselves despite our parents' ongoing worries.

That winter, Ronnie and I came up with an ingenious way of keeping warm. There were Chinese vendors who cooked yams in potbelly stoves and sold them on the street corners. We would each buy two of them and stuff them in our coat pockets to keep our hands warm; we would then go to a movie and slowly eat the yams as we watched. What wonderful warmth they gave us, inside and out!

Mama and I went to the Russian Orthodox Cathedral quite often. I especially remember going to vespers, when the whole interior of the church was dark except for a few flickering candles. My grandmother would send me with prayer books for our well-being and memorial prayers for the souls of our family's dearly departed. After arriving at the church, I would stand in the corner of the huge sanctuary—Russian churches do not have pews—and absorb the quiet mysticism of the moment, before the parishioners crowded in and the choir began singing.

On one such evening, I had gone to the church early, and as I walked in, I saw Archbishop John standing on a dais on the right side of the church. He was dressed in a plain black cassock, and he was praying. He was a small, frail man with a sparse, dark beard and long hair. Within a few minutes, the altar boys approached him and began laying elaborately embroidered brocade vestments on him. The ritual mesmerized me, and as I watched, I felt a strong bond to old Russia that I had somehow not realized until that evening.

Mama was increasingly anxious about her parents in northern China, as she had not heard from them for many months. She had recently discovered that the letters she had been sending her parents were going unanswered and lost, which meant that they had vanished during transport. Mama came to learn that the Chinese had taken the area surrounding Harbin, where her parents lived, expelling its previous Japanese occupiers; the region was in chaos, and any contact had become utterly impossible. She hoped and prayed that the Klukins would not fall victim to the ravages of war.

When American forces dropped an atomic bomb on Hiroshima, Japan, on August 6, 1945, we heard about it in Shanghai. Three days later, they dropped another one on Nagasaki, and we heard about that as well. We were amazed to learn about this new thing called the "atom bomb"—and that a single such bomb could destroy an entire city. However, we did not know the true devastation that these bombs had caused until after the war ended, when we heard all about it from the Americans.

The shock of the atom bombs had only a temporary hold on us, however, for along with this tragic news came a glimmer of hope. We heard people saying that these bombings meant that the end of the war was certainly very near, and to my family, even such rumors were welcome. Just like everyone else in Shanghai, my parents were tired of being cold and hungry, tired of not having decent opportunities to work for a living.

In August, finally, our hopes were confirmed when Japan's Emperor Hirohito went on the radio to announce that World War II was officially over. Everyone in Shanghai—Japanese, Chinese, and White Russians alike—listened intently to the broadcast, and when we heard the words we had waited so long to hear, the streets erupted! The Chinese, who had of course never liked the Japanese occupying their land, went out of their houses and threw firecrackers; they also threw stones at Japanese businesses in retaliation for the years of oppression they had suffered. Japanese officials refused to acknowledge that the war was really over; they insisted it was just a rumor. Their determination not to accept defeat deflated the festivities a bit but did not deter the Chinese from their joyous celebrations in the streets.

In a day or two, we were all relieved to find that the war was truly over. I was elated, of course, though my parents and my grandmother were not able to let themselves be too happy about it just yet. As for myself, I was anxious about the future as well.

"What will happen now, Mama?" I asked. "Can we stay in Shanghai? Are they going to make us leave?"

Mama smiled at me as she washed the dishes from that evening's dinner. "I'm not sure, Olinka," she told me gently. "We will just have to wait and see."

"But what if they send us away? What if they make us go back to Japan?" I asked, my anxiety becoming quite obvious. "What if we have to live somewhere *even worse*?"

"Olga, Olga," Mama said, drying her hands on a towel and coming over to hug me. "Don't worry. Wherever we go, we will all be together. And as long as we're together, everything will be alright."

"Okay, Mama," I said, giving in to her hug, even though I remained a little bit nervous about the situation. We had moved so many times already, and even though I did not love Shanghai, at least I was used to it. Who knew how bad the living conditions would be somewhere else? *Only time will tell*, I reminded myself, and I tried to be patient as we waited to learn what our fate would be at this newest turning point in our lives.

Chapter 9:
After the War

The U.S. Forces Arrive

A few short weeks after World War II was officially over, the Japanese began to pack up and leave Shanghai, and the Americans arrived. We were all happy to see them, and we greeted them with open arms—they truly were our liberators. They brought us freedom and hope.

We soon learned that through the American consulate, we could apply for visas to the United States. We did so without hesitation—along with every other foreigner in Shanghai. We were put on a waiting list and told that they might get to us in two or three years.

Not everyone's wait was so long, however. My friend Ronnie and his mother were able to leave Shanghai for Australia in 1947. This was a great loss to me, of course; Ronnie had been my best friend for several years, and I was heartbroken over losing his companionship.

Right after the war ended, all the English and Americans in Shanghai were repatriated to their countries. This included my old teacher, Mr. Gardenstein, who was British. From what I later heard, when offered the chance to go back to his home country, he left immediately, but he refused to take his wife along. He harbored resentment about the affair she had with the Japanese official, even though it might have been what saved his life throughout the war. However, he made his decision, and he filed for divorce and left without her.

I saw Mr. Gardenstein one last time before he left the city, and as a parting gift, he gave me a thick volume of Jane Austen, a complete collection of her work.

"Read every word of it, Olga," he told me. "Once you understand the whole book, you can consider yourself a master of the English language!" I was so excited about this present and set to reading it immediately. Over the years, I treasured that book, and I read it over and over, thinking of Mr. Gardenstein every time I opened it up.

We also heard a bit of news about our beloved Chizuko after the war. Through Luba, my godmother, we learned of a rumor that Chizuko had survived the war, and what's more, she had married a Chinese man and had a child. Mama and I tried for a while to find our old friend, but we were never able to make contact, though we continued to hope that the rumors we had heard about her were true.

There were plenty of new people in our lives as well after the war. The building across the street from ours—the one where Papa had almost rented an apartment when we first arrived in Shanghai—had long ago been commandeered by the Japanese and turned into a military hospital. When the Americans arrived, however, they took over the building and made it into a U.S. Army hospital. My brother went over there right away to look for a job, and he was given one in the X-ray department; he made many friends and soon began bringing American GIs over to our house. My parents even rented a room out to soldiers who needed somewhere to stay during their days off.

We had two or three different American military men coming and going in our apartment at all times; needless to say, the bathroom line was quite long some mornings! My parents began to pick up a few useful English words and phrases from our interactions with the GIs, who were enthusiastic about teaching them simple conversational terms. Mama started cooking lunch every day for six to eight people. It was certainly a busy time in our home.

I had a crush on one of the soldiers who rented our room from time to time, a young man whose name I cannot remember now. But he was handsome and friendly; he took me to see newly released American movies at the military barracks a couple of times a week. I was thrilled to see Rita Hayworth, and I adored Gene Kelly and Frank Sinatra in *Anchors Aweigh*. The GIs gave us packs of records as well, and before long, I knew every popular American song by heart.

The atmosphere in Shanghai was charged with optimism and energy. Businesses that had closed during the war now returned, as well as the stock exchange at the Bund. Jobs were plentiful and money began to flow. Many Russians found employment with the U.S. military, including Valia and her sister, who were elated with their jobs at the Army commissary and canteen.

Above: Me, age 14.
Below: Me on the street near our house, age 14.

The Russians in Shanghai

Although many people left Shanghai when the war ended, the Russian community and the commerce it had built over the years still thrived and even grew. Before and throughout World War II, this community was split into two uneven factions: the White Russians and the Soviets. The Soviets, who were far less in number than the White Russians, were often looked down upon, or even outright despised; many White Russians saw them as traitors against their poignantly remembered home country.

During and especially after the war, the Soviet consulate established itself in Shanghai to promote its political agenda. The Soviets' purpose was clear: they wanted all of us to go "back home." They showed propaganda films and put great pressure on the community, and many actually succumbed to their tactics. My parents were surprised by how many Russians in Shanghai were receptive to the Soviets' ideas. It seemed that some people, especially those who lived in poverty, thought their lives would improve in the Soviet Union, and the appeal of going back to Mother Russia was very strong.

Despite this controversy, however, my family had friends on both sides. We knew one family in particular, the Belkins, who bought into Soviet propaganda. My brother dated their youngest daughter, Ida. She was a bright young woman, a tutor, and she did not in any way share her family's sympathy for the Soviets. It was, of course, a great source of dissent within the Belkin family.

It did not surprise us to learn that Ida's family applied for Soviet citizenship. They sold almost every one of their possessions and used the money they made to buy clothing and canned goods, supplies that would last them a long time. The Soviet government sent a Russian passenger ship to Shanghai to bring the returnees back to the U.S.S.R.; I believe there were about 2,000 Russians on that ship. The Belkins and my teacher, Tina, were among the passengers, and when it was time for them to depart, my family went to see them off. It was a sad farewell. We did not hold any optimism for their future.

Some time later, we heard that the Soviet government, which assigned jobs and living arrangements to all citizens, had placed most of them in Siberia. In letters the Belkins sent to my parents, they mentioned that many of their belongings had not made the entire journey with them. They hinted that they had regrets about leaving Shanghai as well. Ida most certainly was not happy in Siberia, but we heard that eventually she was able to go to Moscow and a better future, perhaps.

We knew others who gave in to the Soviets in return for the privilege of returning to their country. A friend of Mama's, a professional woman, actually divorced her husband to become a Communist, so that she would be able to go back to the homeland. We saw many people leave, though some had many apprehensions. My family and I, however, simply continued to wait in limbo, stuck in Shanghai until the American government decided what they wanted to do with us.

Chapter 10:
Shanghai at Limbo

Russian Orthodox Easter

Easter is one of the most important holidays to any Russian, though for the White Russians in Shanghai in 1946, it was perhaps *the* most important holiday of the year. Throughout World War II, we had kept great focus on our religion; just as it had been in the homeland, the rules and rituals were an integral and emotional part of most Russians' lives. We deeply revered the Church, which has always been a very strong cultural part of being a Russian. As Leo Tolstoy said, "faith was the force of life" in Russia.

Our first Easter after the end of the war was a great time for festivities. There was a sense of the religious observance coupled with the celebration of our own freedom, our own hopes for the future. Easter traditionally welcomed in the spring season and reminded us all of the annual renewal of life, and there was definitely a feeling of revitalization during that time in Shanghai.

In keeping with the Russian Orthodox tradition, we first observed the long seven weeks of Lent. This was always a solemn time, but during the last couple of weeks, as Easter grew closer, households began to bustle with preparations—cleaning, changing the winter linens to the spring ones, and of course, cooking. We happily made vegetable dishes with the produce that was abundantly available since the end of the war; we also made Easter breads called *kulichi* that took almost a whole day to bake, and a cheesecake-like delicacy called *pas-ha* (see recipe at the end of the book). There were piglets and lambs to roast, eggs to color, and many other delicacies to prepare. On top of all that, daily church attendance was expected.

Palm Sunday was observed by carrying v*erbi*—pussy-willow branches—in place of palms, a custom that began long ago, when palm fronds were not readily available in the cold climate of Russia. To us, pussy willows were a true symbol of spring, as they were the first trees to break out at that time of year.

The last week of Lent was a culmination wherein we fasted and continued with our daily church attendance. On the Thursday of that week, there was a long evening service that lasted three or four hours. I remember standing in the magnificent Russian Cathedral in Shanghai on this night, listening in wonderment to the choir singing and chanting the psalms and the New Testament. The choir always sang *a cappella*, as the Russian Church does not permit musical instruments. Many great Russian composers wrote church music.

At the noontime service on Friday, the *plaschanitza*, a large, beautifully embroidered sheet of cloth that symbolized Christ's burial shroud, was carried in a procession around the church. The parishioners who bore it then placed it in the center of the sanctuary and adorned it with embroidered linens and beautiful flowers. It would remain there until we commemorated the time of Christ's resurrection the following night.

On Saturday, an hour before midnight, we all dressed in our best clothes and filed into the Cathedral for the Easter service. Feverish anticipation ran through the congregation as we all stood closely together, holding unlit candles, quietly listening to one of the church officials reading aloud from the New Testament.

Exactly at midnight, the altar candles were lit and the church bells began to ring as the doors to the altar opened and Archbishop John emerged. He was followed by his retinue of a dozen priests and many altar boys, all dressed in magnificent celebratory vestments; the group led the parishioners outside and around the Cathedral, as was the custom. Then, the choir began to sing glorious Easter music, and the priests called out, "Christ has risen!"

"Indeed, he has risen!" we answered. Easter had finally arrived! Elation took over as the clergy and the entire congregation walked around the church to share with each other the traditional Easter greeting, three kisses on the cheeks. My parents looked happy as they kissed their friends and shared a few words of camaraderie. I held fast to my mother's hand, enjoying listening to the choir's continued singing and smiling whenever someone bent over to wish me a happy Easter, especially the two or three GIs we had invited to witness this auspicious celebration.

When this joyous moment was over, some people rushed home to break their fast. Others who were more religious stayed at the church until the end of the service, at 3 a.m. We stayed about an hour only, and then we hurried home, carrying our candles with us; it was good luck to bring a lit candle home from church. Because it was faster than walking the several blocks to our apartment building, we decided to take a rickshaw home. Mama had to make sure that her table was laid out and ready for the many visitors we would receive, including several U.S. soldiers.

The tradition for Easter night was to eat, drink, and be merry until sunrise. People would go from home to home, visiting friends and relatives and partaking of the delectable dishes each of them offered. This year, the hostesses' tables presented hams, roasted piglets, and lambs; beet salads, herrings pickled with onions, mushrooms in sour cream, caviar, and potato salads; the tall *kulichi* breads, cheese *pashas*, and most important, colored eggs. Children stuffed themselves with chocolate eggs and bunnies. For the adults, the vodka, liquor, and wine flowed freely.

At our apartment, we all sat around our big table—Mama and Papa, Luba and Volodya, Valia, me, and our GI guests. Though we were all eyeing the delectable food on the long table that Mama had prepared—it had certainly been a long period of fasting!—we took a moment to raise toasts to the holiday and to each other.

"Happy Easter, everyone!" Volodya exclaimed, raising his glass high in the air. "Let us toast to the end of the war, and to the happiness this year has brought upon us all."

"To new friends," announced one of the American GIs, and everyone laughed and cheered.

"To a better future," added Luba, smiling brightly and raising her glass as well.

"To a better future *in America*!" said Mama, and we all cheered, especially the GIs. At that, everyone clinked their glasses together and drank, and then we dug into what we had all been waiting for—the food!

One young GI who joined us that night had never eaten Russian food before, and he enthusiastically piled his plate with all we had to offer. As he was getting second servings, I saw him reach across the table to one of our small crystal dishes. He removed its lid and seemingly without consideration for what it even was, put a big dollop of the dish's contents on his plate. He settled himself, all ready to enjoy this feast of new tastes. I sat across from him, cracking open some beautifully colored eggs.

"Enjoy your meal!" I said to him cheerfully, and he nodded in return, already with a loaded fork halfway to his mouth.

First, he took a bite of lamb, closing his eyes as he chewed, as if he had just died and gone to culinary heaven. "Oh," he said, "that is *delicious*!" Then he tried some potato salad, and his throat emitted a pleased sounding, "Mmmmm!" Spurred on by these wonderful tastes, he dug into the unfamiliar substance he had found in our covered crystal dish and popped it into his mouth.

From across the table, I could see his gustatory elation vanish. Tears welled in his eyes, and his cheeks turned pink as he struggled to keep the unexpectedly spicy food in his mouth. I put a hand over my own mouth to stifle my giggling.

Finally, the GI got up enough nerve to swallow, which led to a round of rather violent coughing. When he recovered, several minutes later, he saw that I had been watching him, and he asked me rather pointedly, "What *is* that stuff?"

"Why, it's horseradish," I told him. "My father made it himself—it's one of his specialties. Don't you like it?"

"Like it? It nearly killed me!" he said, smiling as he wiped a napkin across his perspiring forehead. "Next time I find something here I don't recognize, I'm sure going to ask you what it is before I put it in my mouth."

"That's a good idea," I told him, pouring a glass of water from a pitcher in the middle of the table. "Drink this," I said, handing it over to him. "It may help."

He thanked me and guzzled the water down, then with a satisfied sigh, he continued eating, steering very clear of the horseradish from then on.

These festivities continued for several days; there was a lot of eating, much drinking, and great happiness all around. This was the first Easter after the long and difficult war. Easter was the holiest and most joyous holiday in Russia—a celebration of warmer days, when the snow melted and the ice broke on the rivers and lakes. It was a time of renewal, a time for new life to begin. It was this sentiment that we White Russians clung to during our Easter celebration in Shanghai. By that time, we were all certainly ready for a new phase of our lives to begin.

For several weeks after the holiday, it was Russian tradition for the clergy to visit and bless the homes of each person in the congregation. During this time, I was stricken with pneumonia and was bedridden for some time. When it was our family's turn to receive the clergy, we were delighted to find Archbishop John himself at our door. As Mama and Papa welcomed him inside, he saw me lying in bed, weak with the illness. He came over to me and smiled kindly.

"Do not worry," Archbishop John told me softly. "You'll be fine."

The next day, my brother, who worked at the U.S. Army hospital across the street, brought a nurse and a doctor to examine me. They immediately administered penicillin, which at the time was a miracle cure for pneumonia and other maladies. As I began to feel better, I began to think that Archbishop John's blessing was indeed a miracle in itself that brought that wondrous medication to cure me.

Summer Sets In

On June 16, I celebrated my 13th birthday. I planned to have a party and invite all my friends, and I was fortunate enough to be able to have a dress of my own design sewn especially for me by a tailor. It was made of peach-colored lace, with a full skirt and puffy sleeves. As I tried the dress on, Mama noticed for the first time that my posture was not correct, that I seemed to be standing with one hip lower than the other. She later brought me to Dr. Ivanoff for an opinion on this and we found out that I had scoliosis, though it thankfully did not develop into a debilitating condition.

I became even closer with my friend Klava around this time. When she did not have homework to do, I would hop on a streetcar and go over to her apartment, where we spent a lot of time together. She had a neighbor, three doors down, named Tony, a 15-year-old, gorgeous Italian boy whom we both had enormous crushes on. For a time, our favorite pastime was to stroll down the alley outside Klava's apartment building; I would sing popular American songs so that Tony might hear and come outside to see who we were. Unfortunately, to my great disappointment, he did not pay any attention to our crooning, even when we sang right underneath his first-floor window. He completely ignored us, but for some reason, we persisted with our endeavors.

Another Death in the Family

By the summer, my grandmother's health had begun to deteriorate rapidly. In July of 1947, her kidneys were failing, she was retaining water in her body, and her lungs filled with it. She required medication every day, and she was absolutely bedridden in her glass-enclosed room. Up to this time, she had been keeping herself busy with darning, sewing, and any cooking tasks that could be done at the table, but after her health worsened, she was unable to do anything but lie down, propped up on pillows, and rest. Valia, Volodya, and Luba—Grandma's three favorite friends—came often to comfort her. Volodya valiantly tried to cheer her with his collection of silly jokes.

Before long, Dr. Ivanoff quite reluctantly gave us the news we had all been waiting to hear. "I'm sorry," he said, speaking quietly to Mama. "There is nothing that I can do to improve Paraskeva's condition. The end of her life was approaching. But Faina, she is in so much pain all the time, I wonder if this is even for the best."

Mama nodded solemnly, thinking immediately of how she would tell my father. "Thank you, Dr. Ivanoff," she said to our old family friend. "We will do what we can to make her last days comfortable."

On the night before she died, she called me over to her bedside. "Olinka," she said, "take out my earrings and keep them as a memory of me." My grandmother always wore a lovely pair of coral and gold earrings, the only treasure she had left from Russia. I carefully unhooked the earrings with my trembling hands, then clasped them in my fists; I fought back tears, realizing that at last, she would not be with us much longer. I took Grandma's hand and smiled at her, and she smiled back. She looked peaceful, even though she labored over every breath she took.

The next day, in the middle of the afternoon, Papa and Mama sat on Grandma's bed and I stood alongside, watching her slow breathing. Then, at last, there was a final puff of breath, and it was all over. I clearly remember a breeze gently blowing the window's curtain, but otherwise it was so very quiet. It was the first time I saw someone die. With the help of a nurse who had also been in attendance, Mama washed my grandmother, as was Russian tradition. They put her in a clean robe and laid her down.

"Look how well she looks now," Mama whispered as she stood next to the bed, explaining to me how in death, Grandma's body had relaxed. She no longer looked arthritic and bloated; she seemed to be at peace. We buried my father's mother in Shanghai Cemetery. She was 73 years old when she passed away.

Around the time of my grandmother's death, another family tragedy had begun to unfold. My mother had not been able to get in touch with her own parents for some time. They still lived in their little cottage, out in the middle of nowhere in the northern Chinese province that I visited with Mama in 1937.

In June of 1946, Mao Tse Tung's Communist forces began their advance in Manchuria, where his soldiers engaged in frequent skirmishes with Chang Kai Shek's army. One night, these various troops retreated in the middle of the night in the vicinity of my grandparents' house, and some of them decided to break in and loot the place.

The first thing the soldiers did was kill the trusty old German shepherd sleeping in the kitchen, whose bark had awoken my grandparents in the next room. Then they burst into the old couple's bedroom and tied them to their bedposts. As the soldiers ransacked the house, they kept taunting and beating my grandparents. They turned every room upside down and found no large amount of money, which seemed to be what they were searching for.

"Take anything," my grandfather cried as they hit him. "Take everything!" The soldiers demanded money from him and continued beating them both, pummeling my grandmother's head repeatedly against the bedpost. They hit her so hard and so much that they eventually cracked her head open, and brain matter began to ooze out, a very painful detail that my grandfather told me some 20 years later.

Eventually the soldiers ran out of the house with jewelry and silver, though there were a few hidden Russian heirlooms that they missed. Grandpa tried unsuccessfully to escape from his bonds; grandmother hung limp on the bedpost as she lost consciousness. Grandpa called for help as loudly as he could, hoping that anyone outside might hear him. Their Chinese neighbors, who had always been nice people, eventually, as they saw the soldiers depart, came to investigate and found them in the bedroom. The neighbors untied them both, but they could tell that Grandma was in dreadful condition. They

Olga Valcoff

gently laid her down, unsure of what to do about the entire situation.

Once he was untied, Grandpa reached out to his wife, slumping down on the floor next to her. He picked her up as best he could and held her in his arms, weeping and rocking her gently, kissing her bloodied face. He told her how much he loved her and held her unconscious body until she passed away.

The neighbors took my grandfather to a hospital that was a few hours away. He begged them to contact his only relative in Mukden, a nephew, to notify him of the tragic events and to ask him to come and bury his beloved wife. The nephew did come, and he took care of the funeral matters that Grandpa was unable to attend to, as he was still in the hospital. Grandpa never found out if the attackers were Mao's or Chang Kai Shek's soldiers, or if, perhaps, they were just marauding bandits looking to loot innocent citizens. My thinking, however, is that they were a band of loosely knit soldiers that belonged to one party or the other.

Grandpa eventually recovered from his physical injuries, but he was certainly never the same after the trauma and tragedy he suffered. He closed up their house, having no desire to live in it alone and be reminded every day of what had happened there. His nephew took him back to Mukden and gave him a place to stay.

All this while, Grandpa kept sending letters to Mama to tell her what had happened to her mother, apparently to no avail. Desperate to get in touch with her, in the fall of 1946, he took the advice of an acquaintance and put an advertisement in a local Russian newspaper in Shanghai.

"Looking for my daughter," it read. "Faina Shlyapin, lives in Shanghai. Urgent!" He included the address of where he was living at the time, hoping that Faina, or at least someone who knew her, would write to him.

This idea turned out to be a great stroke of luck. Mama saw her father's advertisement in the newspaper not long after it was printed, and her elation was immeasurable. She immediately sent a telegram to the address he had provided, telling him where she lived and what was going on in our lives. Grandpa answered quickly to tell Mama what had happened to him; when Mama read this letter she just crumbled onto a chair. She was inconsolable, worse than she had been when she had received the news about her sister, Nina. Papa and I did our best to comfort Mama; he helped her write a letter to her father, imploring him to come to Shanghai, and they sent him some money as well. She desperately wished that he would leave Manchuria, which was by then under Mao's Communist control.

No sooner did he receive Mama's invitation than he packed his few belongings and left town on the last trainload of refugees. He arrived in Shanghai on September 3, 1947, the day after the funeral of my father's mother. Despite all he had been through, when we met him at the station, he smiled; to my eyes, he was physically strong but gentle, and he seemed to be the same kind and thoughtful person that I remembered. He hugged each of us as though he did not want to let us go, telling us all how happy and relieved he was to see us. In that small way, he gave voice to what we were all thinking—that during this new difficult time for our family, we were thankful to at least be together.

1947: Change Is In the Air

At the end of 1947, the U.S. Army started leaving Shanghai little by little, jobs were hard to find, and the postwar euphoria was quickly dissipating. Though Mao's armies were slowly spreading throughout the country, many White Russians would not believe that the Communists would take over all of China, and especially not Shanghai. Others, however, feared the worst and looked for ways to leave before any such shift in power could take place.

During the first couple of years after the war, Mama's friend Valia and her sister, Mara, dated only American GIs. They hoped to find their knights in shining armor, but unfortunately, they did not have much success. Mara ended up marrying a Serbian man, and they moved to the U.S., leaving Valia behind in Shanghai.

Valia did not find an American husband either, leaving her to face a future that seemed rather bleak. She decided to marry a Ukrainian man, though the union was for security, not for love. He was coarse and plain, not a pleasant man at all, and Mama had a great deal of apprehension about the marriage. We all loved Valia, and it was obvious that he was not a good match for her.

One day, Valia came to our apartment looking very distressed. It seemed that she had recently been contacted by the father of her daughter, Margie, who had returned to his native Holland soon after the end of the war. He wanted Margie to live with him and finally take on his last name.

"What should I do?" Valia asked my mother. "I know that it would be better for Margie to live with her father. He's rich, and she would be free to grow into a proper European lady. I don't have much to give her, but I love her so much. She means more than life to me!"

Mama shook her head solemnly. "I don't know what to tell you," she said quietly to Valia, holding her friend's hand. "What a difficult decision. I could not imagine sending Olga away like that, but then again, if it meant that she would have a better life… Well, I just don't know what I would do, Valia."

Eventually, she agreed to send Margie to Holland. It was an enormous sacrifice for Valia; it left her feeling bereft and depressed, despite her recent marriage. Soon after the little girl left, Valia and her husband were able to leave Shanghai, and hoping to start a new life once again, they moved to Brazil. My family lost a very dear friend the day they left, and unfortunately, we never saw Valia again.

A Last Vacation

In the summer of 1948, I was given the opportunity to travel outside of Shanghai. My mother had friends who owned a villa in a mountain resort town called Moka Shan, and my brother and I were sent there to stay with them for a while.

Moka Shan sat in a chain of mountains near Hang Chow. I traveled there alone, as my brother had job responsibilities and would follow later. I took a day's journey by train, then a bus to the foot of the mountain, and then a three-hour sedan-chair ride up the mountain itself. I was carried through some very narrow passes and some very high precipices, as well as through a bamboo forest. It was certainly an exciting experience being carried over precipices and mountain gorges.

The town that was my destination was perched on the very top of this mountain. It had once been a popular vacation spot for rich Chinese and Americans, but when the Japanese began to take over the land, they claimed it over for their own uses. The architecture of the town consisted of three varieties: exquisite, dilapidated, and bombed out. After I was there for a few days, and had time to explore, I found a sort of castle with a wall around it; it was empty, and thus a perfect place for me to sit and read the complete collection of Jane Austen to my heart's content. The view on one side of the wall was a plateau, while the other side showcased the mountains, and I changed seats every time I visited so that I could take in all the beautiful surrounding scenery. I did a lot of reading there.

When my brother arrived, I went hiking with him and some of his English friends, who had made the trip as well. We picnicked in a valley by a river; when we jumped in for an afternoon swim, we found that the water was icy cold. The mountain air, however, was magnificent—crisper and fresher than what we were normally subjected to in Shanghai.

The Chinese people who lived in Moka Shan told us that there were tigers around, but that they went away from people in the summer. One day, a couple of the local people took us to a tigers' den, where we saw droppings on the ground, as well as hair that the tigers had shed. However, there were no tigers in sight. I had hoped to see one up close, but in my heart, I was secretly glad that I was not afforded that opportunity.

Wild boars were also known to come into the town at night, from the northern side of the mountain. Usually it was an enormous male that came calling under the wall that surrounded the town, snorting and digging his way in. Because of this, we were always careful when walking outside at night and made noises to scare away any boars that might be lurking about.

There were ferocious yet spectacular lightning storms on the mountain that we would watch, mesmerized. There were many beautiful things, such as the very fragrant, wild lilies that grew in the waterfalls and brooks on the mountainside. They bloomed in lilac, yellow, pink, and white, and I would sometimes take dangerous chances crawling out to crevices to pick these flowers. Best of all, I had not been bothered with asthma, and my breathing was easy.

Perhaps 1948 was the last year of freedom in China, because the next year, the Communists moved in. Even though I did not know this at the time, I relished my visit to Moka Shan as though it were a reprieve from imprisonment. Though I missed my parents, my return home was reluctant; I wished I could have stayed longer. However, when I returned to Shanghai, I found that the respite had been good for me, and I felt ready to face whatever was presented to us next.

Goodbye, Shanghai

The political situation in Shanghai grew worse by the day, with Mao's forces advancing rapidly throughout China. It became obvious that the city would fall to the Communist party, and panic understandably ensued.

The Russian Immigrant Association of Shanghai, whose leaders were trying to organize a mass evacuation, contacted the International Refugee Organization for some assistance. The IRO was a special division of the United Nations that was established in Shanghai to help people of various nationalities who wished to emigrate as political refugees. With their help, many went to live in South America, Australia, New Zealand, and various European countries.

After several months, there were seven or eight thousand White Russians left in Shanghai who were trying to go to America, including my family. In addition, more White Russians streamed into the city from Tsintao, Harbin, and Peking every day, all looking to once again escape the encroaching threat of Communism.

My family—and the rest of the White Russians in Shanghai—were told by the IRO to dispose of our property and belongings in preparation for our exodus to a safe, interim place. Terror and anguish gripped us all. Where would we go? Who would want us? Remaining in Shanghai was out of the question, as we would face deportation to the U.S.S.R. as soon as the Communists occupied the city. Any Russians who were thus forced to return to Russia could have faced execution as anti-Communist traitors; others could have been sent to gulags or subject to general extermination. We were trapped in fear and despair, scrambling to dispose of our possessions quickly and at great cost. The greatest example of this was our apartment, which we would have been able to sell any time before for $15,000. Now, we felt lucky to have gotten only $1,500, furniture included.

The old French military barracks in Shanghai were commandeered to accommodate all the White Russian residents, as the IRO needed us all to be located in one area. We stayed there for about four weeks, during which time my brother found out that he alone was approved for a United States visa. He had recently turned 21 and was able to apply for one to fulfill a Japanese quota—because Japanese nationals were not allowed to emigrate to the U.S. at the time, the U.S. filled their visa requirements with people who were born in Japan but were not citizens. It was a gray area, but it worked out well for my brother. Within a few weeks, he left for America by himself.

The rest of us—my parents, my grandfather, and I—learned that we would be sent to a refugee camp in the Philippines. Our departure was hasty, which was fine, as we looked forward to getting out of Shanghai. When the IRO told us it was time to leave, we took our few suitcases—the rest of our crates would be shipped separately—and boarded the airplane they provided, eager to start what we hoped would be the final chapter in our ongoing saga of statelessness.

Chapter 11:
The Philippines and Beyond

Hello, Tubabao

View of the Tubabao camp.

The International Refugee Organization had secured us a space in a camp they were building on Tubabao, a small island in the Philippines. A group of White Russians had flown out there in December of 1948 to prepare the area for inhabitants, to rebuild whatever was left over from its former days as a U.S. military encampment during the war. They arrived expecting to see a fairly intact facility, but all they found instead were Quonset huts that had been torn down by storms and scavenged by natives who lived in other areas of the island. The IRO quickly sent an assortment of U.S. Army tents, stoves, cookware, and other supplies, and in addition, U.S. military food rations.

The Russian construction crews worked as quickly as they could, and as soon as a section of the camp was sufficiently set up, they sent for refugees. The more they built, the more people came; in all, 6,300 people ended up in Tubabao, and most of them were White Russians like my family and me.

Having a good time dancing

The four of us, along with Luba, Volodya, and about a hundred or so refugees, left Shanghai for good in January of 1949. We flew to the Philippines on a prop plane, with our belongings following us by ship; our first stop was in Manila. We had been told to wear lightweight clothing for the trip, as the weather in the Philippines was decidedly tropical. However, we were not warned how cold it would be on the plane, and we were shivering the entire way there. When we were finally allowed off the plane in Manila, it was like stepping from an icebox into an oven, but we were happy for the warmth after such a long, chilly plane ride. Unfortunately, we had to stay in the airport all night while our paperwork was processed, making us official wards of the Philippines, under the supervision of the IRO. None of us slept for even a minute.

The next morning, we flew from Manila to Samar. The view was spectacular as we flew over the multitudes of islands in the early morning, which gave me hope that life on the island may prove to be pleasant, perhaps. We then went by bus on to Tubabao, the island that was to be our temporary home.

Our social entertainment square.

The camp we lived in consisted of U.S. Army tents and a few quickly constructed plywood buildings that took advantage of the former Quonset huts' cement foundations. My family had two small tents joined together; we all slept on old army cots surrounded by mosquito netting, my parents in one tent and my grandfather and I in the other. We assembled a makeshift covered dining room on one side with a piece of tent material that we attached to the sides of tents; Grandpa and Papa built benches and a table that helped to make our setup a little more homelike and comfortable.

The camp was broken up into several districts, each with its own kitchen, and the adults all had to take turns on KP duty. Everyone had to stand in line for meals, which we would then take back to our tents to eat. We were mostly served soup, noodles, rice, and some particularly unappetizing beef stew, though we occasionally had a little cabbage or potatoes as well.

Though our quarters may have been sparse, in time the camp grew to be a truly thriving town. We had a church, a school, and a community stage where the residents staged plays and concerts and showed American movies. There were frequent dances and beach parties that many young people enjoyed. As a teenager, I found that life in Tubabao certainly provided much fun and a busy social life. As a bonus, the tropical weather seemed to be good for my asthma, as it hardly bothered me at all the entire time I was there.

Klava and me in Girl Scout hats.

My old friend Klava had ended up in Tubabao too, and we happily continued our friendship in this new, foreign land. In addition, I made new friends, including Valentine

Bagdassarian, who was for a time my closest girl friend. Val and I—and sometimes Klava—spent all our time within a small group of boys and girls. We enjoyed a great deal of social outings together, including trips to the beach, movies, parties, and especially the dances that were held often on Saturday nights. We loved listening to the popular American songs and learning new dances, such as the jitterbug.

Valentine and me.

Soon I met George, who was the first boy I was ever interested in romantically. He was athletic, he played the piano beautifully, and he was a good dancer—everything a girl could want. He was a driver in the camp motor pool, so we always had a Jeep to run around in, which was great fun. We often went to the beach to swim and watch the sunset. As well as the moonlight. I fell head-over-heels in love with George. I thought he felt the same for me and we were meant for each other forever.

The Philippines had some of the most beautiful sunsets I have ever seen; each one featured different colors that filled the sky and reflected off of everything around us, bathing us in its hue. As we sat in the sand and enjoyed this show of nature's beauty, the air was filled with the scent of tropical flowers, which grew abundantly and in wide variety all over the island. It was truly an amazing sensory experience that I still enjoy revisiting in my mind to this day.

Olga Valcoff

In front of our "dining room."

Ups and Downs of Camp Life

Life in Tubabao was generally one big party for many young people, but for the adults in our camp, the atmosphere was entirely different. Some were depressed because of the climate, which was often oppressively hot. We had to contend with monsoons and typhoons that in turn caused mudslides on occasion. Many of the older people were chronically despondent because they thought they had come to a dead end, seeing no future for themselves and their families in the Philippines. Former businessmen now spent their days fishing and dejectedly reminiscing about their previous lives, which had been busy with work and wealth. Other residents fared better, involving themselves in a variety of chores and occupations to deal with the daily routine of life in the camp.

For the first year or so that we lived in Tubabao, my father's mental stability, which had never been the same since his incarceration, held out all right. He had his bouts with depression, but nothing worse than he experienced in

My 17th birthday party.

Shanghai. He remained active in the community; he was even put in charge of a hot-water station, which he managed enthusiastically.

Later on, however, as people we knew started to leave for various countries, Papa showed a steady decline. Watching the camp begin to empty out made all of us a little dejected, but it affected Papa the most. He began to spend entire days brooding; sometimes it was almost as though he lived in another world altogether. He grew paranoid and at times expressed his distrust of my grandfather, with whom he had previously shared a wonderful relationship. Friends of our family told Mama that she should take Papa for help, which she reluctantly agreed was the best thing to do.

Saying goodbye to Val when she departed to Australia

With Volodya's help, she convinced him that everyone had to get a physical examination by the camp doctor, and though he was suspicious, he consented to go. However, as they walked him through the camp toward the doctor's office, he tried to run away, and his "physical" was never completed.

Papa started to accost our neighbors and scare people in the camp, and though I hate to say it, I was embarrassed by his behavior and concerned greatly for my mother, who was constantly looking after him. Before long, she could no longer keep up with him, and with great sadness in her heart, Mama had my father committed to a medical facility. He stayed there for a few weeks—from December 12 through January 6—and we were allowed to visit him every day.

Mama brought him food, as he would not eat anything that came from anyone else. When friends went to visit him, Papa would seem happy and calm, but as soon as they left, his mind would snap back and he would think he was still living in the "good old days" in Kagoshima. After a while, Mama didn't want me to visit Papa, though I did anyway.

Once people began to get their visas and leave Tubabao, it was like a landslide. People were leaving in groups, to Australia and to North and South America. More than half of the camp emptied out in one year—by the middle of 1950, less than 3,000 people were left in our once overpopulated town.

My boyfriend, George, got his visa for the United States about a year after living in the Philippines. He and his family were overjoyed, but of course, I was crushed. On our last night together, I cried as though the world was ending, and the next morning, I went to see him board the plane that would take him away from me forever. Once he was inside the aircraft, I stared blankly at it, feeling nothing but shock. Soon after the plane departed, my friend Valentine took me aside.

"Listen," she said to me confidentially, looking around to make sure we were alone. "He's not worth it."

"What—what do you mean?" I sniffled, tears welling in my eyes.

Val sighed dramatically. "Olga, he was carrying on behind your back with another girl. She gave him what you would not do!" she said angrily, referring to a girl that was in our group of friends. She used to chase George—it was very obvious—but he always assured me that he had no interest in the girl, that he was utterly and completely faithful only to me.

In an instant, I felt my tears dry right up. "Why, that…!" I said, suddenly seething rather than crying. We left the airfield and I immediately put my mind to forgetting all about George. It only took me three or four days to get him out of my heart and mind. He was my first love and the knowledge that he was carrying on with someone else was very painful. I felt deeply wounded and betrayed, and I became very angry.

Not long after that, Val's parents became disillusioned with waiting for U.S. visas and they decided to head for Australia instead. This was another sad parting for me, as Val had been a very close friend. However, in retrospect I can say that some good did come out of it, because in Val's absence, my friendship with Klava grew much stronger.

Our Time to Leave Comes, But...

Late in 1950, a bill was passed in the United States that granted permission to any Russians left in Tubabao to immigrate to the U.S. For this bill, we had to thank Archbishop John, who persuaded Senator William Knowland of California to take action on our behalf and essentially push it through Congress. Soon after this happened, people began to leave much faster.

Senator Knowland visiting our camp.

Though Papa's growing mental instability had been difficult for us all to deal with during our stay in the Philippines, at that time, it presented a new problem. Not too long after the U.S. visa bill was passed, our applications were processed, and we were then thoroughly scrutinized by American consulate officials. We were made to undergo thorough health examinations, which both Mama and I passed without a problem. Papa, however, ultimately was not approved because of his mental condition. As a result of the physical, we were informed that instead of joining the rest of us on the boat ride to America, he would be sent to an institution in Germany.

My friend Klava did not pass her doctor's examination either. Some spots were found on her lungs that were indicative of the beginnings of tuberculosis. Because of that, she was denied entry to the United States. Klava's entire family—her father, two brothers, and mother—had already received their permissions to leave, but due to Klava's condition, they were forced to split up at that point. The two boys left for the U.S. as planned, along with their father; Klava's mother stayed behind to take care of her daughter while treatment for her condition was arranged. Eventually Klava's mother was able to make plans for her to go to Tokyo and stay with good friends they had there and take treatments for tuberculosis. Once these arrangements were made, Klava's mother went to the U.S. to join the rest of her family, and Klava was flown to Tokyo. She stayed there for about a year, until the spots were gone from her lungs. She was then able to go join her family in San Francisco.

Though my mother had gained admittance to the U.S. without a problem, as we prepared to leave Tubabao, she became distraught, desperately wishing to go to Germany with Papa instead. She did not feel right about leaving him alone and wanted to be there to take care of him.

"But Mama," I told her, "there is nothing you can do to make him better. You and I can have a better life in America. Please, come with me!"

"Oy, Olinka," she cried. "He is my husband. How can I leave him behind?"

"I know you love him, Mama," I told her gently. "I love him too. And there is no doubt that he loves both of us as well. Mama, he would want us to be happy. He would want you to fulfill the dream that you both had, even if he cannot do it with you. We've suffered so much, we deserve some lasting happiness. Come to America with me, Mama, I need you, too! We'll make a home for ourselves there, at last."

Mama spent much time tearfully debating the situation with herself, but in the end, my pleas worked. We left for the U.S. in January of 1951 aboard an old Army transport ship. My grandfather unfortunately did not join us, as he had recently suffered a stroke and was in a hospital in Manila; he was to join us in the States when he recovered, which would be about six months later. Such was a reality of many families that were fractured, as Klava's and ours.

Setting Sail on the U.S.S. Haig

*Waiting to board the USS Haig.
I am in the foreground frowing and mama
In a kerchief next to me, on the right.*

Our boat ride to America was not exactly what we had expected. We boarded an old, rusty U.S. military transport ship with minimum amenities. Mama and I were placed in steerage, the lowest level of the vessel, which housed another dozen or more women per section as well. During the voyage, the ship was caught in a very bad weather pattern; many typhoons raged in the Pacific Ocean, and though the captain tried to steer around the storms as much as possible, he could not avoid them all. This made our trip longer than it had to be, and many passengers were positively green with seasickness.

My mother fell victim to the boat's unsteady sailing. She vomited constantly and remained lying on her cot for most of the trip. At one point, a sailor on the ship's crew mentioned to me that grapefruit had been known to alleviate nausea, so I helped myself to an extra one at breakfast and smuggled it back to the room for Mama. Though the sour taste was difficult for her sensitive stomach to take at first, after managing to eat some of the fruit, she did feel her seasickness wane a bit. Fortunately, I was lucky not to have had any seasickness during the trip. I was free to enjoy the good food prepared by the ship's cooking staff, which some of us were invited to partake of in the officers' quarters.

We first stopped in Honolulu, where we were not allowed to go ashore, to my great disappointment. From the deck of the ship, I could see the island's beautiful beaches, and even a few surfers off in the distance. I would have loved to have disembarked and spent a few days there. Alas, it was not to happen at that time, though I mentally put Hawaii on my list of places to visit sometime in the future.

Hello Golden Gate — Goodbye Russia

Aboard the ship, nearing San Fransisco

From there, it was another few days to San Francisco, California, our final destination. The weather had improved and our sailing was much smoother. Mama's seasickness did subside a bit, but she was still feeling its residual effects when it was announced to us all that we were approaching San Francisco.

"Mama!" I said, rushing to her bedside and shaking her gently. "Get up, Mama! We're almost there!"

"Almost where, Olinka?" she asked me sleepily.

"San Francisco," I told her excitedly. "Please, try to get up." I picked up her slippers from the floor and struggled to put them on over her heavy socks. "Don't miss this moment, Mama," I told her as I helped her dress for the outside weather, which she hadn't felt for many days. "We've been waiting for this for so long!"

I bundled my mother up in her coat and scarf, then did the same for myself. I put an arm around her and hoisted her up off the cot; she was weak and thin, as she had undoubtedly lost weight due to her constant illness. I escorted her directly out of the room and up the few steps to the deck, and even this short task was a great effort for her.

When we reached the deck, we found it crowded with most of the other passengers. Everyone looked anxious, staring into the dense, enveloping fog that surrounded the ship as though waiting for a vision to appear. The foghorns were hooting a deep-voiced greeting, an announcement that we were approaching land. Mama and I stood there shivering in the damp, penetrating cold, unable to see anything, clutching each other, anticipating the frightening future. Everything around us was perfectly still, not a sound except the bellowing foghorns and the whoosh of the waves against the ship's hull.

Suddenly, a strong gust of wind came in and blew away the fog, and it was as though a curtain had opened to reveal an enormous, panoramic window with a most breathtaking view. Directly before us was the Golden Gate Bridge, a huge, orange vision, its arms outstretched as though offering us a hearty welcome to America.

The people around us on the deck began to cry and shout with joy, hugging and kissing their families, friends, and even perfect strangers in their happiness. Some ran to the deck's railing to toss coins into the water for good luck, and I thought that was an excellent idea. I reached into my coat pocket, where I had a few pieces of U.S. currency jingling around.

"Here, Mama," I said, handing her a dime and keeping one for myself. "Make a wish!"

Mama smiled at me; for the first time since the start of this voyage, her cheeks were rosy and she seemed almost back to normal. She took the coin from my hand and squeezed her eyes closed, making her silent wish. When she opened them, she nodded at me and we tossed our coins into the water together.

"Olga," she said, "I can't believe we're finally here. Our journey has been so long—for me, it's been 50 years! It's just so hard to believe that it finally might be over."

I hugged my mother tightly, unable to speak because of the sob that was stuck in my throat. She was right—our family's journey through Asia had been long and sometimes unbearably difficult, and the feeling of knowing that we would no longer be on the run—that we would no longer be stateless—was indescribable joy to us at that moment.

As the ship slowly glided underneath the bridge, I felt an enormous thrill; it was as though we were passing through an actual gate, opening a path that led to our new home. I felt a great camaraderie with the other passengers at that moment, and with all the refugees of the world; I hoped that they would all eventually find their places in the world, and that all their journeys ended as happily as mine did.

I was 17 years old when we arrived in San Francisco, and though I had never been to Mother Russia, I was reminded every day of my heritage and my culture. No matter where we lived, no matter what befell us, my family persevered and kept the traditions alive. Throughout my life, I have carried in my heart the precious memories of my family's brave journey that began so long ago in the distant Ural Mountains, and the battles we all fought while searching for a place to call home—a home called America.

Epilogue

Shortly after Mama and I arrived in San Francisco, we continued our journey to Seattle, Washington, where our dear old friends Panya and Sasha met us with open arms and lots of love. We settled there, and about three years later, Mama opened a Russian restaurant called Troyka, which did very well.

In the course of her business, Mama became friendly with one of her customers, a Russian gentleman named Peter Tulintseff. Upon obtaining a divorce from my father, Mama married Peter.

After living in Seattle for a while, I returned to California to attend college; later on, I moved to New York City. In 1962, I went to Germany to visit my father, where he lived in an excellent institution. Though he did not recognize me, he kept telling me about his beloved, 14-year-old daughter, so I knew that somewhere within his mind, he remembered me and the better times we had shared. It was difficult for me to spend a couple of days with him, but I am glad I did it. He passed away in 1965.

In 1966, I met and married Nicolas Valcoff, a man of Russian descent; he was from France but had immigrated to the U.S. Later on, we moved to New Jersey, where we still live today. We have one son, Nick, and a beautiful granddaughter named Natasha.

In 1969, my mother and Peter moved to New Jersey to be near my husband and me, and especially their beloved grandson, Nicky. Peter died shortly after. My mother lived with my family and me from 1984 on, until she passed away in 1999 at age 96.

Japan Revisited

Dear reader:

After 67 years, I returned to Japan. A good friend, Kenji Harahata, who lives near Tokyo, was most instrumental in a plan to visit my old childhood friends in Kagoshima. He contacted the main local newspaper inquiring if there was a way to find anyone who would remember me and my family. To my great luck, a delightful and energetic young newspaperwoman, Miss Nakano, was assigned to do the project, and wrote a couple of articles about my story.

Well, to my great surprise, people began contacting her, saying that they remembered me and my family when they were children and lived in the neighborhood. One man, Mr. Yamakuchi, called in saying that he is the little boy in the photo of the newspaper (see page 64) Imagine his surprise? And mine as well! One thing led to another, and it became clear to me that I needed and wanted to undertake this trip.

Therefore, on Oct. 16th, 2006, I took a 14 hour plane ride to Tokyo from Newark Airport. Yes, 14 hours! My friend Kenji was there in Tokyo to greet me. I stayed in the area called Shinagawa in a nice hotel near the train station. What a pleasure it was to see everything so immaculately clean and orderly! That evening I had a delicious Japanese dinner which was the first of many that would follow throughout my stay in that country. After a very good sleep, I woke up next morning well rested.

That morning we took an 11 o'clock flight to Kagoshima. I was indeed very fortunate to have Kenji accompany me on my journey. He was truly a Knight in shining armor, helping me at every step, as well as translating, since my Japanese is very limited today.

My eyes started misting with emotion at the thought that I was finally coming back to a place I was born, though the city has changed completely. Many buildings have been destroyed by Allied bombing during the WWII. At last we arrived at the hotel which was built on the same street where I lived. The streetcars were still there though they were modern and in variety of colors, not the brown wooden ones I remembered. After I freshened up, I came down to meet Miss Nakano and Mr. Yamakuchi and his wife, as they insisted on seeing me the first day. As soon as I stepped into the lobby he rushed towards me. We both were crying as we hugged each other. It seemed that we had seen one another just a short time ago, not the many years that have passed. After we calmed down he and Kenji were anxious to show me the house I lived in. I expected to walk perhaps a few blocks, but as we went outside, Mr. Yamakuchi turned me around and pointed at the hotel "This is where you lived!" he said. I was astounded. The original building was demolished long ago and a new one was built on the same spot. My friends had conspired to surprise me. They certainly did! The same evening, Kenji and I invited Miss Nakano to dinner. Kenji had selected a very good restaurant, and the three of us had a fabulous Japanese feast. I brought Miss Nakano a gift. A teapot made in Russia that I brought in my carry-on luggage without breaking. She was very pleased to receive it, and while looking at the teapot she accidentally dropped the lid, and broke it. Well, the damage was small and repairable.

Next morning we were invited to a luncheon with the five people who were my pals from the kindergarten. Two ladies and three gentlemen. We spent a delightful afternoon reminiscing about our school days and having a delicious Japanese meal. It was very touching to have these people take time to come to see me. One gal had to take a train early from Fukuoka to come to Kagoshima.

That same night I received a spectacular evening at the home of Yuriko Uno who is a teacher of traditional Japanese dancing called Odori. She served a sumptuous dinner; platters and platters of various Japanese specialties that were beautifully arranged. After the dinner Ms. Uno gave a presentation by her students with Odori dances, that were followed by a Koto lute player, Ikebana flower arrangements and finally a teacher who showed me the art of calligraphy.Ms. Uno wanted to show me the scope of Japanese classical arts.

I was deeply touched by this gesture. In fact, we didn't know each other except through correspondence for a few years. To top it all, her two lovely students dressed me in a gorgeous silk kimono and wrapped me in a brokade obi that was finished off with a beautiful bow in the back. I tried to dance a little with a fan, which Ms. Uno gave me at the end of the evening. And what an evening it was!

My second day's schedule was to have a luncheon with seven former neighbors. They selected a restaurant in a hotel on the hill above the city, overlooking the bay and the volcano Sakurajima.

Seeing these people again, who once were my little play mates, brought on a flood of emotions and a deluge from my eyes. I was glad to wear waterproof mascara that day. The outpouring of affection, their sweetness and pure joy at seeing me I will never forget. Mr. Yamakuchi was less than four but he remembered a great deal and said that I was the tallest of the bunch. What made it the most special for me was seeing Kinuko-chan; a small, pretty and youthful looking woman. In fact, everyone looked very well and energetic. When we settled down to lunch we began exchanging memories and stories about our youth. Gifts were exchanged as well.

The day flew fast and it was time to say those "I'll be seeing you again" Goodbyes. Alas, probably never!

Mr. Yamakuchi offered to take Kenji and I sightseeing. We decided that it was a good day to go to the volcano. We took a 15 minute ferry ride across the bay. The ride around the mountain was spectacular as the road circles the island close to the water providing a gorgeous panorama. We saw many traditional houses which have fishes with their tails up, perched on each end of the roofs that is unique feature of this area. We drove as far as the old Torii gate that was nearly submerged by the lava ash after the eruption of 1914. Yes, it's an active volcano. As we arrived at the top of the overlook point, Sakurajima puffed out a big smelly cloud.

It was a pretty sight by the time we returned as it was already evening and the city was lit up. The Yamakuchis live in Japanese style house where we spent a pleasant time having dinner and looking at some old photos. I am so fond of Mr. Yamakuchi as he is a sweet, kind and affectionate man. Fighting tears he told us about an early death of his sister Toshiko at age 29. She is the girl in the middle of the picture on page 64.

On the fourth day we spent the entire time with Kinuko-san, lunching, shopping and sightseeing. We went to Iso Goten, a 350 year old samurai Shimazu family villa, near the bay with the view of the volcano, of course. I felt sad that at the end of the day I had to say "I'll be seeing you again" to Kinuko-san.

On the fifth day Miss Nakano accompanied us to the 90th anniversary celebration of my kindergarten that the missionary Miss Finley established in 1916 with only five children. Now the enrollment is near 300 and all are Protestant Christians Japanese. After the musical presentation there was a slide-show tribute to Miss Finley, her life and accomplishments. To my big surprise the school principal announced "Among the guests there is a former student who went to our school in 1936, Mrs. Olga Valcoff"

I stood up to an ovation, fighting my tears. It was wonderful to be a recipient of so much affection! After leaving the kindergarten, we said goodbyes and many thanks to the lovely and intelligent Miss Nakano; who during my 5 day stay in the city wrote articles about me everyday.

I think she will have a great career as a reporter.

Kenji and I took a short train ride to Miyama, a village of Satsuma Pottery famous for over 400 years. The potters pass their knowledge from one generation to another. We went to the studio of the most famous one, Chin Jukan the 14th who is 80 years old and is a National Treasure. We went to just look at his prized pottery only when after a short time that gentleman appeared and Kenji began a conversation with him.

He asked us to have tea with him. He was fascinated that I was born in Kagoshima and returned after many years. As we were leaving, he presented me with a teacup from his studio. That was an honor, indeed.

The next morning was a time to say a sad goodbye to my beloved city and the wonderful people I was fortunate to be with. It was the best and most emotional experience in my entire life.

We flew to Kobe a little over an hour's flight. A business associate of Kenji joined us and we spent an afternoon walking around the district of Kitano-cho where I lived. We tried to find my house. Alas it was gone and a "Wedding Palace", I think was in its place. To my big surprise though, I found the house where Helen of the "there's no Santa Claus story" lived and my Indian friend Razilia's house was still there. They are now museums of the old town.

I went to Razilia's house trying to conjure some memories. It was raining all day and by late afternoon it began to pour. However we bravely walked down the hill to our hotel. Later we went to the Daimaru Department store which I remember well. I bought a box of Morozoff chocolates. We hada final Japanese dinner where I bought an expensive bottle of sake for my husband and received two bottles of sake as well as gifts.

On my final day in Japan, Kenji and I took a train to Kyoto. Ah, those marvelous Japanese trains, one can set a watch by them. In the morning we went to see the old Imperial Palace. Then at lunch time we were joined by three Kenji's friends. Having a brief lunch, I went to the Golden

Temple and Heian Shrine where the magnificent gardens were.

At the shrine I saw a lovely Maiko-san, a young geisha that became a subject of my photography. Having walked so much that day it was difficult to sit down at the tatami style restaurant that evening. The ladies that accompanied me that day were very charming and I hope to continue my friendship with them.

At last we had to leave for Tokyo by the bullet train that should have taken 2 and a half hours. Well, the train was delayed as someone jumped in front of the train to commit suicide. Amazingly, all the trains were systematically delayed without an accident.

On this last night in Japan Kenji treated me to my first non-Japanese dinner at an elegant French restaurant.

Next morning it was time to say goodbye to this amazing country.

And "thank you" to my dear friend Kenji Harahata for this enchanting journey.

Recipes

Panya's Blinis

6 cups flour—sifted
5 cups milk—warm
1 cup water—warm
1 package dry yeast
½ stick butter (1/8 lb.)—soft (room temperature)
3 tbsp oil
½ tsp salt
2 ½ tbsp sugar
4 eggs—separated

1. Combine yeast, ¼ tsp sugar, 1 tsp flour, and 1 tbsp warm water in a cup. Set cup in small oven; let rise and bubble.
2. In a deep pot, combine ¾ cup of flour, 1 tsp butter, 1 tsp sugar, and 1 very hot (almost boiling) cup of milk. Add the yeast mixture. Set on a warm tray, cover with a small blanket, and let stand until it rises a little (about 20 minutes).
3. Add 2 cups of flour and 1 cup of warm water. Let stand 10-15 minutes.
4. Add egg yolks, butter, oil, sugar, salt, the rest of the warm milk, and the rest of the flour. Let stand 2 hours or more. Cover and keep warm.
5. Just before cooking, add whipped egg whites and let stand 10 minutes.
6. COOKING: Use cast iron, small-sized and medium-sized frying pans. Melt 2-3 tbsp of butter. "Paint" the

pans with the melted butter with a brush. Pour a large serving spoonful of dough onto the very hot pans at high heat. Let dough bubble to a light brown color; flip the blini over for a minute or less.

7. Serve blini either with sour cream or smoked salmon, other smoked fish, or caviar (red is okay); marinated herring is also appropriate. Chilled vodka is more than appropriate.

Mama's Katletki (beef patties)

2 lbs. lean ground beef
1 egg
½ cup plain breadcrumbs (plus some extra for dusting patties)
2 tbsp soy sauce
½ medium onion, grated
2 tbsp chopped dill or parsley
2 tbsp vegetable oil
Black pepper to taste
Dash of sweet paprika
½ cup or more of water
Ice cream scooper

In a large bowl, moisten the breadcrumbs with water. Add all ingredients except the meat. Blend well. Start breaking the meat up into small chunks and blending them into the bowl using a large fork, adding water bit by bit. Using an ice cream scooper, take two scoops and make them into oval patties. Dust each patty into the remaining breadcrumbs. Repeat, and either refrigerate or freeze. This takes 45 minutes or less, and makes 8 or 9 patties.

Add vegetable oil to a nonstick pan and fry the patties slowly. Non-frozen patties should take about 15 minutes, frozen ones 25 minutes.

Easter Pas-ha (Mme Valcoff)

6 lbs. farmer cheese
2 lbs. butter (unsalted)
12 egg yolks
2 vanilla sticks
1¾ lbs. sugar (extra fine)
¼ cup sweet almonds
¾ lb. candied fruit
½ pint heavy cream

Preparation
Scrape vanilla sticks; set aside.
Set almonds in hot water; remove, peel skins, and cut in very thin slivers. Set aside.
Cut candied fruit in small chunks; set aside.
Strain farmer cheese and butter twice; store mix in large bowl.
In separate bowl, gradually mix sugar with yolks. Then gradually mix in vanilla.
Return to large bowl containing farmer cheese and add gradually (while mixing manually): egg yolk, almonds, and candied fruit.
Whip heavy cream and gradually add whipped cream to pas-ha.
Refrigerate pas-ha in a receptacle that allows drainage. Use cheesecloth to line between receptacle and pas-ha. Russians use a pyramid-shaped receptacle, but otherwise, use a clean, new, clay flowerpot.

Printed in the United States
108228LV00004B/85/A